Scars On My Heart

S.L. STERLING

SCARS ON MY HEART

by

S.L. STERLING
©January 2024

Scars on my Heart

Copyright © 2024 by S.L. Sterling

ISBN: 978-1-989566-70-1

Paperback ISBN: 978-1-989566-78-7

Harcover ISBN: 978-1-989566-69-4

Editor: Brandi Aquino, Editing Done Write

Cover Design: Thunderstruck Cover Design

About the Book

Willow Valley had become like home to me and my two boys, Dylan and Noah. Everyone knew everyone in this small town, and they helped us heal from our devastating loss.

Once I knew my kids would be okay, I started looking for work. Bluebird Books hired me almost right away. I was to run the new kids program that Trinity was starting. That was where I met Zach and his daughter, Grace.

Zach was the new owner of the Willow Valley Inn. He'd come in to return a book his daughter had borrowed from the program. We exchanged pleasantries and that was when the computer had gone down. Zach lost his patience, and that was when our pleasant conversation turned sour. I wasn't worried about it because I figured I'd never see him again.

I was wrong. It turns out in a small town, everyone sees everyone almost daily, if not twice a day. At the grocery store, the gas station, the elementary school and as luck would have it, the bookstore. Soon, our conversations turn pleasant again, and without even trying, I find myself drawn to him. Then he asks me out on a date.

Despite my reservations, I decided to take a chance on love again. But just when things start to look up, Zach's ex-wife suddenly reappears, causing chaos in his life once more. Which somehow causes chaos in mine when my children begin acting out.

Leaning on one another for support, we navigate obstacles that life throws at us. As time passes I begin to wonder if another chance at love will bring us closer together or make each one of us run the other way?

"Tag! You're it!" Noah yelled from the hallway. Dylan went running by me, almost knocking the box of glasses from my hand.

Frustration built inside of me as he looked behind me, a huge smile on his face. "Sorry Mom, gotta go hide," he whispered and took off toward the pantry in the back of the kitchen.

"Ready or not!" I heard Noah yell.

I set the box of glasses on the counter and began placing each one in the sink of hot water I'd just run. We arrived in Willow Valley yesterday. Now the actual work began, and it looked like it was going to be all on me. I'd just placed the last glass in the sink and was crushing the box when the boys ran back through the room. This time, Dylan caught the leg of one of the chairs and sent the box of dishes I'd placed there crashing to the ground. I cringed at the sound of breaking glass behind me and turned to see him standing there looking at the mess on the floor at his feet.

"Sorry, Mom. I didn't mean to..."

I could see the tears fill his eyes, and hoped I could stop the meltdown before it began. I took a deep breath. The last thing I wanted was for him to cry, he'd cried enough in the past couple years. Besides, there was no use getting angry. The damage was done.

"It's alright." I looked over at the mess on the floor. The last three years had been hard on us all. This was the first time I'd seen either of these boys laugh, and I didn't want to see it end over something so small. "I have an idea. Why don't you take your brother into the backyard and play catch? I found the ball and your baseball gloves in a bag last night and I put them by the back door."

I walked over to check out the damage. I had no clue what was in the box, but by the look of the broken glass spilling out of the top, some severe damage had probably been done.

"Sure." Dylan plodded toward the back door, head down.

"Hey...it's just a couple of broken dishes, nothing that can't be replaced. Okay." I smiled.

Dylan said nothing, just nodded his head. "I'm really sorry, Mom."

I'd tried hard not to get angry with them over the little things anymore. It wasn't worth it, even though my patience was wearing thin, given how tired I was. Since we'd lost Lucas, nothing had been the same. Today was the first day the boys were actually running around laughing and smiling since I'd announced we were moving. They lost their father, and now, because I couldn't afford to keep the house we'd been living in, they were now losing all their friends.

I sighed, bent down, and straightened up the box that had fallen. The instant I saw what was written on the side, I wanted to cry. It contained not only a pile of plates but the two wineglasses that we used to toast on our wedding day.

I closed my eyes as I opened the box. I'd been in a hurry to pack this box and had shoved those glasses down beside the plates, knowing they should have been better protected. On top was a sea of broken plates, and I reached in and grabbed one of the glasses, carefully unwrapping it, producing a perfect glass. When I reached in and grabbed the other, I didn't even need to open it to know it had broken. I'd heard the crunch.

"Dammit," I whispered under my breath as a tear ran down my cheek. The glass was broken, just like us.

"Mom...Mom...." I heard Dylan yell from the back door.

I quickly wiped my cheeks and placed the wrapped-up

broken glass into the garbage. I took a drink of water to help the tightness in my throat.

"Yeah, what is it?" I yelled, my voice not wavering one bit. I'd gotten good at that over the last five years, so many nights I'd spent the evening crying, first when the diagnoses came in and after he'd passed when memories flooded me. Never once had I let on to them that I'd broken down because I knew I had to remain strong.

"There are a couple of kids outside. Can we go down to the park at the end of the road and play?"

I glanced out the kitchen window to see Noah out front talking with two boys who weren't much older than Dylan.

"I don't know..."

"Please, Mom...please. We will just be down at the end of the road. We'll be home by dinner. Promise. Please."

"Alright, well, just be careful. Don't talk to any strangers, and make sure you come home on time for dinner. You have your watch?"

Dylan held his arm up and pulled his sleeve up, showing his watch.

"Okay, no later than five," I said, glancing up at the clock.

"Thanks, Mom. Again, I'm sorry about the box."

He kissed my cheek quickly as he passed through the kitchen and took off out the front door.

"Alright, boys. Dinner is ready!" I yelled up the stairs where they had been tasked with making their beds. It had been a blessing to have my brother-in-law and his friends available to be here for the movers yesterday. They had been kind enough to set up all the bedroom furniture for us, so I didn't have to.

I was just plating their food when I heard their footsteps scramble down the stairs and into the kitchen. I carried over their bowls and placed their meals down in the front of them.

"Spaghetti?" Noah questioned.

"Yes," I answered. "I am tired. It was easy."

"Ah, Mom, but you promised pizza tonight," Noah cried.

"I know I did. How about we have that tomorrow, okay?" I said, scooping some pasta into my bowl. I grabbed the garlic bread from the oven and placed it in the centre of the table before sitting down across from the boys.

"You promise?" Dylan questioned.

"Yes, I told you, we'd order from the same place I used to get pizza from when I lived here as a young girl."

"You really grew up here?" Noah asked, scooping up a

spoon full of noodles and completely missing his mouth, pasta falling down the front of his shirt and onto the floor.

"Yes, I sure did. Do you remember passing by the flower shop when we drove into town?"

Both boys thought for a moment and nodded.

"I grew up in the house behind that. Not too far from here. Willow Valley was smaller then. This house didn't even exist when I grew up here. It's grown a lot since I left."

"Why did you leave?" Noah questioned.

"Well, I met your dad at school, and we moved to the city."

"Are we going to go to the same school you went to?" Dylan asked.

I nodded. "Yep. Willow Valley Grade School. You are both going to make lots of friends, and I think you will really like it here. Willow Valley also has lots of town activities. They have the fall fair and winter activities, like skating on the lake and a winter festival."

"I miss Billy," Noah whined. "We were the best of friends. It's not fair we had to move." He dropped his spoon into his bowl and crossed his arms across his little chest, scowling. "Now all I have is my brother."

Once again, I could see the tantrum about to start. Noah was eight. It hadn't only been a long day for him but for all of us, and the last thing I wanted was for him to act out. I was about to say something when suddenly Noah had spaghetti hanging off his face and head. Dylan burst into laughter as I glanced over at him.

"That is enough. Eat your dinner. Don't throw it at your brother," I scolded.

Just as I finished giving Dylan crap, he now had spaghetti hanging off his face, and Noah let out an infectious giggle. I glanced over at him, ready to yell, but suddenly they both were smiling and laughing, which caused me to laugh.

The next morning, I stood in the kitchen, unpacking more boxes as both boys played video games in the living room. It was a new house and none of us had slept well last night, so I was trying to keep it a low-key day for all of us. My phone vibrated against the kitchen counter, and I reached for it as I placed the glasses I'd just washed in the cupboard to the left of the sink. I opened my email and was surprised to see a response from the job I'd applied for before bed last night. I skimmed the email and smiled to myself.

"Boys!" I called.

"What?" they both called back.

"I've got some news. I got a job," I said, sitting down behind them on the couch, excited to share this news with them.

"A job?" Dylan questioned.

They had never seen me work. Lucas and I had been fortunate that he'd had a good job that enabled me to stay home with them. I'd done my best to maintain that the last couple of years, but there had been some events that had eaten into our savings. The sale of the house had fortunately paid for this one, and it gave us a bit of a cushion which I'd been grateful for. The life insurance money that Lucas had, I'd decided I wanted to use for the boys' education, which meant I'd had no choice but to get a job.

"Does that mean you won't be home much?" Noah asked, dropping his controller to the ground, on the verge of another breakdown.

"Well, it means that I will work outside of the home, just like Daddy used to. However, the hours will coincide with school once you start, so you won't notice as much. However, there will be times during the summer that you will be home here with a sitter and not with me," I said, trying hard not to break down in tears as their sad eyes looked up at me. They'd seen me cry enough in the past year, and I'd vowed to myself to be stronger for them, especially now that we had moved.

"Where are you going to be working?"

I patted the cushions on the couch next to me and waited for them both to sit down beside me. "Well, there is a small bookstore in town here, run by a woman I used to go to school with. She will be, or I should say is starting a young readers program, and with my volunteer hours that I accumulated at the young readers' program at the library back home, she was pleased to offer me the job. That means you both will get all the books you want to read, you'll get to meet new people, and while you do that, I will make money to support us."

"Will you be making enough that we can have an allowance like before?" Dylan questioned.

I swallowed hard. Lucas and I had given the boys a tiny allowance. Now money would be tighter than before, and I wasn't sure if I'd be able to. I shook my head. "We will have to see, okay?"

Dylan nodded, clearly not happy with that answer.

"I promise, guys, things are going to be okay." I wanted to be reassuring, but I knew my voice was anything but.

"I miss Dad," Noah said, leaning into my side and wrapping his arms around my waist.

"Me too," Dylan said, wrapping his arms around me from the other side.

I wrapped my arms around them and pulled them in for a hug. "I know you do. I miss him too, but you know what? He'd be so proud of the two of you for making this move and how well you are adjusting. You're both going to like it here so much. You just need to wait and see. Your dad liked it here. Often we'd talked about retiring here."

"Really?"

"Yes," I said, hugging Noah again.

Dylan got up and wandered over to the living room window and looked outside. There was yelling on the street.

"What's going on outside there, Dylan?" I questioned.

"Just a bunch of kids playing basketball."

"Well, why don't you guys go outside and see if you can join in? What do you think of that?"

Dylan looked over his shoulder at me and smiled, running to get his shoes on, followed by Noah.

I got up off the couch and watched as my boys ran down the front steps and out to the road, where they were quickly welcomed and began playing with the other kids. I watched for a few minutes and then quickly replied to Trinity, letting her know I was excited to hear from her and to get the start date for my new job. Then I slowly made my way back into the kitchen and continued unloading boxes.

An hour later, I'd made a cup of tea and sat down in the kitchen with a sandwich to take a break. I looked around at the piles of boxes that were strewn about. It was going to take me forever to get this house organized. I guess it was just going to take one day at a time. That was all I could do. I really hoped I hadn't made a mistake by moving out here. Sure, it was a quieter life, but the jobs just didn't pay what they paid in the city. However, neither were mortgage prices.

Taking a sip of my tea, I sat back in my chair. "Lucas, I really hope you are watching over us up there. I could really use your help," I muttered, before taking a bite of my tuna sandwich.

"Grace, sit still, would you?" I said, struggling with her hair in one hand and an elastic band in the other.

"That isn't the way Mom does it! You're pulling my hair," she cried, tilting her head away from me.

"Well, it's not Mom doing your hair now, is it?" I grumbled, irritated that I couldn't get the elastic to cooperate with my big fingers. Finally getting the elastic around the messy ponytail, I took a deep breath and committed myself to the next challenge. "Now hold still while I figure out how to braid your hair."

"A braid is easy, Dad." Grace sighed.

I'd been watching YouTube videos for days on how to braid hair, and even though it appeared easy, it really wasn't, and I struggled with how to hold her hair. Grace sat in front of me, running her spoon through her oatmeal.

"Why do I have to eat oatmeal? I don't even like oatmeal. Mom would never make me eat oatmeal."

"Since when don't you like oatmeal? It's good for you. Now eat it before it gets cold. You can't go to school without breakfast."

"Mom never makes me eat oatmeal," Grace said, taking her spoon, holding it in the air, and watching as the oatmeal fell back into the bowl.

I'd known full well this would be what happened after Grace stayed with her mother for the last couple weeks of summer, while I came out here to look at this property my mother wanted to buy. We'd recently lost my father, and it had always been her dream to run a bed-and-breakfast. So, with nowhere to go after my divorce, I figured I'd check it out with her. Turned out to be a deal we couldn't turn down, and with my investment in the property, it left my mother with only a tiny mortgage.

"Grace. Please. Just eat your breakfast. I have a lot to get done today. The contractors will be here soon to start renovations in the rooms, and I need to get you to school."

"I told you; I don't want to go to school. I want to stay here with Grams."

I was ready to bang my head against the wall.

"Well, you can't stay here with Grams. Now why don't

you want to go to school?" I questioned, finally finishing the braid and securing the bottom with an elastic.

"I don't like what I'm wearing."

I was ready to call Valerie up and give her a piece of my mind. I swore she'd made this child act this way on purpose. Sure, she was eleven going on seventeen. Despite that, she'd never been this argumentative before. She'd literally gone from a wonderful, polite angel to this spoiled brat I could barely handle.

"Well, I'm sorry, but you picked out this outfit in the summer specifically for today. You liked it then. What has changed?"

I knew this had to do with Valerie. No doubt in my mind. Grace shrugged and shoved a mouthful of oatmeal into her mouth, making a face.

"Dad, fashion changes. You'd get that if you were a girl."

There it was! It was like I was sitting across from Valerie all over again, listening to why it was she needed some new purse or something. I let out a sigh, sat down with my bowl and a cup of coffee, and ate, then pulled Grace's lunch from the fridge and packed her lunch bag.

"What am I having for lunch?" she asked while bringing her half-eaten bowl of oatmeal over to the counter.

I glanced down, feeling completely defeated that she hadn't eaten her breakfast. "Ham and cheese sandwich, an apple, a banana, some carrots and celery, and this," I said, producing half a brownie that I'd purchased at The Crispy Biscuit. I watched as Grace's eyes lit up at the sight of the sweet delight. "Go grab your backpack."

Saying goodbye to my mother and with Grace secured in the truck, I climbed into the driver's side and started the engine, waiting for the truck to warm up before I backed out of the driveway.

"Oh, Daddy, I forgot..." Grace muttered.

"What you forget?" I questioned, lifting my head from a message I was sending to a contractor, and glanced over toward Grace.

She held up the book we'd borrowed from Bluebird Books before she'd gone to stay with her mom. Instantly, I cringed. I'd found the young readers' program almost as soon as we'd moved into town. We could borrow books for Grace to read, sort of like the library.

"Grace, I told you to remind me to bring it back."

"I forgot," Grace whined.

I glanced at my watch. I was running late, and if I went to the bookstore first, Grace would be late for school. "Give me the book," I demanded, waiting for her to place it in my hand. I quickly threw it onto the seat beside me and backed out of the driveway.

Once I'd dropped Grace off at school, I made my way through town over to Bluebird Books. I pulled in behind a car, slammed on the brakes and quickly hopped out of the truck and made my way to the door. That was when I realized I'd left the book in the truck. I ran back over and pulled the door open to find the seat empty and the book missing.

"Fuck me...if this day gets any fucking worse, I swear..." I'd thought I'd heard something fall when I'd slammed on the brakes but had paid little attention. I was about to reach between the seats when I heard a small voice behind me. I turned to see an older woman with a stack of books in her arms.

"Sir, is everything okay?" she questioned.

"Just wonderful," I bit out. When I caught the look on her face, I cleared my throat and gave a weak smile. "Sorry, I'm just running behind, and I seem to have misplaced the book I was supposed to return."

She tilted her head to the side and glanced into my truck. "Sir, it's between the seats. It has a green cover, right?"

I turned and spotted the book almost instantly. I pulled it out and looked over at the lady, giving her a crooked smile.

"Little light reading I see?" She softly smiled.

"Oh this. It's for my daughter," I muttered, tucking it under my arm. "Can I carry those in for you?" I nodded to the armful of books.

"Nah, carrying books is good for my bones."

I ran over to the door and held it open for her, waiting

for her to step inside before following. The line inside was just long enough to frustrate me even more. For a small-town bookstore, the place was packed, and I knew I was going to be late.

I pulled out my phone and quickly texted my mother to let her know I'd be there shortly. I blew out a breath, trying to maintain patience as the line barely moved.

"Can I help you?" a tiny voice asked.

I glanced up to see a woman, mid-thirties, sitting behind the desk. Sweat covered my brow as I looked at her. She was pretty, blonde curly hair, large brown eyes. She stood up, and my eyes instantly ran the length of her body.

"I have this to return," I said, handing her the book.

"No problem. Thank you." She softly smiled. "Can I get the name?"

"Zach Thatcher," I responded.

She quickly typed something into the computer and shook her head. "Sir, I'm sorry, but there isn't any record..."

"I mean Grace...Grace Thatcher."

The woman smiled and began typing again when suddenly the store was bathed in darkness. The power had gone out. Everyone was silent, and then a few people began whispering, just as the power came back on.

"Give me a moment, sir. The computer just needs to

boot up," the woman behind the counter said with a smile.

I wanted to scream as my cell phone vibrated in my pocket. I quickly removed my phone and glanced down at the screen, seeing a message from one contractor. Apparently, they were waiting for me to give final approval on something my mother wasn't sure about.

"Is this going to take long?" I barked.

"I'm sorry, it's not my fault, sir. I'm trying, but it seems the computer has frozen," she muttered, frowning as she stared at the screen. "This is beyond frustrating."

I turned my back on her and leaned against the counter, sending a message back to the contractor. I was furiously typing when I felt a light tap on my back.

"Sir, it will only be a few more minutes."

"You are right, this is frustrating," I grumbled. Irritated, I went back to my message, and after a few more minutes, I turned back around and watched as she stared at the screen. "Well?"

A few moments passed before she smiled up at me. "Can I get the name again?"

"Grace Thatcher," I growled while replying to yet another message on my phone.

"Okay. I have it here. Looks like it was a few days late. There is a small fee."

"What for? I thought this was a free program."

I shoved my phone back in my pocket and looked over

the counter at this beautiful woman who I normally wouldn't have taken a tone with. She sat there, a look of concern on her face as she studied the screen.

"Sir, as it was explained to you upon signup, the fees that are charged on the late books are directly put back into the reading program. They go to buy books, which enables us to provide more copies to the young reader program. You did sign the disclosure."

I could feel eyes on me, and my phone was vibrating like crazy in my pocket. "How much?" I growled, now seriously irritated as my phone began ringing.

"Three fifty."

I muttered under my breath as I shoved my hand deep into my pocket and pulled out a handful of change and placed it down on the counter. "Three fifty. Pretty steep fine for a book that is only a couple of days late?"

She didn't answer me. Instead, she focused on picking up the change off the counter.

"What if I didn't pay it?"

"Unfortunately, if you didn't pay for it, then Grace could not use the program anymore. Trinity has some strict guidelines pertaining to the program. It not only teaches the young people to read and understand what they read, but it also is in place to help teach them a sense of responsibility."

I slammed my fist down on the counter. "Whatever," I grumbled. "We probably won't be back."

"Sir...I'm so—"

I held up my hand, stopping her from saying anything else, and turned, making my way out of the small book-store. I didn't want to hear another word. As I climbed into the truck, I answered my ringing phone and pulled away from the curb, screeching my tires. I wasn't sure how this day was going to end, but it had to end better than how it had started.

I was truly at a loss for words as I listened to his screeching tires. I sat behind the counter, staring at the computer screen, fighting back tears. That man just bit my head off in front of everyone in the store, and I had to find some way to compose myself, before I broke down into tears.

"Iris, are you alright?" Trinity asked, holding up her finger to the woman she was serving. "Mindi, just give us a moment."

"Sure thing, Trinity. I can continue to browse a few minutes if that is better."

"Please."

I glanced over at the woman. She had the warmest blue eyes, and I took comfort as she smiled at me. Then she stepped out of line and went back over to the section she'd been shopping in the last ten minutes to give us privacy.

"I'm okay. Nothing like a rude customer to start the day off." I smiled, embarrassed that I'd let someone get to me that badly.

"If you need a minute, my dear, go right ahead and take one. His behaviour was totally unnecessary. There is a pot of fresh coffee in the back, and I think Thomas just dropped off a box of goodies from The Crispy Biscuit. I heard him come in a few minutes ago. Help yourself. They are there for all of us to enjoy."

I nodded, still trying to compose myself in front of the small lines that had gathered in the bookstore.

I wandered to the back of the store and went to the washroom to splash some cool water on my face. I took a couple of minutes to myself, counted to ten, and then stepped back into the hall and into the small kitchen.

It wasn't like me to get this worked up over someone who was clearly having a bad day, but with the lack of sleep I'd had over the last few months, it didn't surprise me. I poured a cup of coffee for myself and Trinity and snuck a small cake bite into my mouth, letting the chocolate sweetness soothe me. I grabbed one more, popping it into my mouth before making my way back to the front of the store.

The rest of the day went by with no issues, and as soon as three o'clock hit, I gathered my things, said good night to Trinity and made my way to my car. I'd just climbed inside and had gotten things situated when my cell phone went off. I pulled it from my purse, worried it was the boys, and glanced at my screen, a wave of relief washing over me. It was my sister, just checking in to see how things were going. I quickly texted her back and went to shove my phone back in my purse when it went off again. I looked once again to see that Dylan was messaging.

> Dylan: Hey mom. We are home. We are starving. Are there any snacks?

I'd gone grocery shopping the day before yesterday and had stocked up on everything. I'd even bought a few extra snacks for the boys for after school when I was working.

> Iris: Yes, in the cupboard beside the fridge. It's loaded with those granola bars you like.

> Dylan: We don't want granola bars.

> Iris: Okay, there are apples and oranges in the fridge.

> Dylan: Mom

> Iris: Alright, what about a peanut butter sandwich split between the two of you?

> Dylan: Mom...

> Iris: Look, I'm on my way home and will bring pizza. Eat whatever you want. There are chocolate chip cookies in the cupboard. Fill your boots.

I shoved my phone into my purse; I didn't have the patience to fight with them or try to get a healthy snack into them today. It had been a week from hell, and I was exhausted. I started the car and drove down to the pizza parlour where I parked the car and took a quick minute to check my wallet to make sure I had enough cash. Then I climbed out and headed toward The Deep Dish. I was getting closer when my cell phone rang, and I grabbed it from my purse.

"Hello."

"Mom, Dylan won't share the cookies," Noah cried into the phone.

I stopped walking and pinched the bridge of my nose. "What is with you two today? Noah, put your brother on the phone."

"Mom wants to talk to you," I heard Noah singsong in the distance.

"Way to go, doofus!" Dylan yelled.

I listened hard as I heard Noah scream, and then Dylan's voice came over the phone.

"What, Mom?"

"Did you just hit your brother?" I questioned, feeling very much on edge.

"No, I just took the phone from him."

"Dylan, I'm serious. If I find out you hit your brother, you're going to be grounded. Now, why are you not sharing with him?"

"I asked him if he wanted some. He said no. So, I ate his..."

I could imagine Dylan standing there with that smug eleven-year-old smile on his face, just egging on his brother. I let out a sigh. "Dylan, I am this close to not bringing home pizza and sending you both to bed without dinner. Now, please, give your brother the cookies, and I will be home as soon as our pizza is ready."

"Dylan...give me....the..." Noah screamed in the background.

I waited, listening hard, only to hear Noah thank his brother. "There, he has them now. Happy?"

I was about to respond when the line went dead. I looked down at my phone, ended the call, and shoved it back into my purse and turned to pull the door open. I walked in, not paying any attention to what was in front of me. Almost instantly, I bounced off what felt like a brick wall and almost fell to the ground, but felt hands grab me before I hit the pavement.

"Oh my god, I am so..." I looked up in time to recognize the man from the bookstore this morning. Zach, that was his name. I stopped speaking and took a quick second to gather my wits.

"Sorry?" he muttered. "You really ought to watch where you are going."

"What?" I bit back. "You were the one rushing on out of the store. Don't you think you should watch where you are going?"

He met my eyes, rolled his, and marched out the door in a huff. I was about to step inside when I stopped. There was no way he was going to treat me like this again.

I turned back around and stepped out into the street, looked both ways but couldn't see him. Irritated, I went back into the pizza place and got in line when my cell phone rang. Reaching into my purse, I saw it was the boys.

"Hello. What's wrong?" I could hear the defeat in my voice after that run-in.

"Mom, do you think you could bring home some pop and chips for tonight?"

I looked at the line at the pizza parlour and let out a sigh. "Sure, I'll go to the grocery store before I order the pizza, okay? So, I may be a little later than I would have been."

"Thanks, Mom."

"Welcome." I shoved my phone into my purse and made my way around the corner to the grocery store. I entered, grabbed a cart, and began making my way through the store over to the junk food aisle. I was about to round the corner when another cart rammed into the base of mine. Irritation growing, I poked my head around the corner and was about to apologize when I caught sight of Zach.

"You again!" I gritted.

This time, a smile fell onto his lips. "Apparently so. Sorry about that. I wasn't—"

"Paying attention?" I grumbled. "Like earlier?"

This time he chuckled. When he wasn't scowling or yelling, he was a handsome man, dark brown hair, blue eyes. He wore a black T-shirt that hugged his body, showing off his impressive build.

"What exactly is your problem?" I demanded. "And what the hell is so funny?"

"My problem?" He smirked, crossing his arms over his chest. When I didn't answer right away, he stopped, and his face started to get a little red. He began to shift from one foot to the other, and then he dropped his arms to his sides. "Look, I'm sorry," he said, finally letting his guard down. "It's been a hell of a day. Shit, a hell of a month, and to be honest, I'm just not really at my best right now."

"Could have fooled me." I shrugged, still feeling a little under attack.

"I think perhaps we should start off on a different foot. I'm Zach," he said, holding out his large hand to me.

"What if I don't want to?" I bit back, watching him. When he didn't move, I finally slipped my small hand into his and gently shook it. "Zach, it's nice to meet you. I'm Iris."

"Iris, nice to meet you," he said, slowly letting go of my hand and meeting my eyes.

"So, what has you all frazzled?" I questioned.

"God, what doesn't. It all started this morning with my eleven-year-old."

Small world, I thought to myself. "You have an eleven-year-old? My oldest just turned eleven a couple of weeks ago. Right now, my boys are home, probably killing each other." I smiled, and we both laughed. I glanced at my watch. I really should grab what I came in for and get back to The Deep Dish. I needed to order the pizza before too much longer.

"Look, I should get going. I've got to get our pizza ordered," I said, reaching in front of him and grabbing two bags of the boy's favourite chips and a bottle of soda.

"Taking pizza home for dinner?" he questioned.

Almost forgetting our run-in only a few minutes earlier, I nodded. "Yep, I promised them tonight would be pizza."

Zach glanced at his watch. "Once I get our pizza, I have to get my daughter. The guy at the pizza parlour said it would be a good fifty minutes. Did you want to grab a coffee while you wait?"

I glanced around at the people passing by. I'd never had coffee with a stranger, especially one who had treated me the way Zach had earlier. However, he seemed to have a lot going on, and he seemed to be a little calmer at the moment. I glanced at my watch. "I guess it won't hurt. I'll go pay for this and then go order the pizza, and I'll meet you at The Crispy Biscuit."

"Sounds good. While you order your pizza, I'll grab us a table."

Ten minutes later, butterflies in my stomach, I met up with Zach outside of The Crispy Biscuit. It took no time for us to get a table and a cup of coffee.

"I don't normally do this," I said, shrugging out of my sweater.

"Do what?" Zach questioned.

"Meet up with complete strangers for coffee."

Zach chuckled. "I wouldn't call us strangers. We are on a first-name basis." He winked. "And you know I have a daughter."

I smiled. "So your daughter, you said she was eleven?"

"Grace. She is a handful. She spent most of the summer with her mother, and to say she has become a little spoiled is an understatement. We just moved here. My mother and I bought the old Willow Valley Bed and Breakfast. We are in the process of fixing it up. There is a lot of work to be done before the place is operational again."

"Wow, so you bought John and Bessy's old place. It used to be quite the place when I was younger. I've heard over the years it fell into disrepair."

"It has. So, you are from around here?"

I shook my head as I dropped two teaspoons of sugar into my coffee. "No, well, I grew up here when I was little. I moved away after college, got married, and had two boys. We just moved back at the beginning of summer."

"Ah, so you are married?" Zach asked.

"Was..." I paused, leaving it at that.

"How old are they?"

"Dylan is ten and Noah is seven. They are my life, and while they love to be boys, I wouldn't change it for the world. Is Grace your only child?"

Zach nodded and took a mouthful of coffee. "She is. She is enough, to be honest. I don't think I could handle another one of her. Eleven going on seventeen. She's a little spitfire."

"Most girls are." I smiled.

I looked over at him and, for the first time, noticed just how blue his eyes were against his tanned skin. He had striking features, and the mop of dark brown hair looked a tad messy, but sexy at the same time. I hadn't noticed how broad his shoulders were or how his shirt had pulled across his biceps either when I'd first encountered him this morning. However, he wasn't yelling now, so it made it a little easier to concentrate on other things.

"So, you're doing renovations to the inn?"

Zach nodded. "Yes, I left my job when I left the city. Divorce has a way of changing people, as I'm sure you know. I packed everything in. My mom caught sight of the place, so she bought the old place, and since I am backing the renovations, we set roots down here. I do not know if we'll be good at running the place or if we'll end up selling it. All I know is that I needed a change. So, I took a leap."

"Wow, that is really brave of you."

"Many of my friends would say stupid. Especially with a little one to look after. What about you? You are divorced as well?"

I took a drink of my coffee and shook my head as I met his eyes. "No, I'm afraid my husband, Lucas, passed away three years ago. He had cancer and had been in remission for about a year. By the time we found out the cancer had returned, it had spread, and it was too late to do anything about it."

"I'm sorry to hear that."

"Thanks, life has a way of throwing you curve balls. It's been an adjustment, but we are getting along okay." I smiled. "The boys and I moved back here, and we are making things work."

"So, you're working at the bookstore?"

I nodded. "Yes, I'm running the young reader's

program. I love working with kids, so there is that. Plus, it gives me something to do when the boys are at school and helps me provide for them."

"Grace loves that program. If only she'd remember to tell me when the books were due. I'm sorry for this morning, by the way."

For the first time, I laughed at the memory of the morning.

"Ah, well, you don't seem like such a bad guy, Zach."

"I'm not. Like I said, it was an off morning." He winked.

Just then, my cell phone rang. I dug into my purse, grabbing it to see my home number on the screen. Instantly, my eyes flashed to the clock just above the counter, and I realized an hour had already passed. I quickly answered the call, let the boys know I was on my way, and hung up.

"That's my cue. I've got to pick up the pizza," I said, sliding my phone back into my purse.

He glanced at his watch. "Now that you mention it, I'm late to get my pizza and Grace," he said, climbing out of the booth.

"Thank you for the coffee."

"Thank you. It was nice to talk to someone other than an eleven-year-old while I try to braid her hair." Zach chuckled, placing his hand on my lower back as we headed out the door. "Perhaps we could do this again sometime?" he questioned.

I turned and looked into those blue eyes of his. "That would be nice. You know where to find me."

"Look forward to it," Zach said as he followed me into The Deep Dish to pick up his pizza as well.

I waved goodbye to Zach, climbed in my car, and headed toward home. It had been nice to go out with an adult, and it had cleared my first thoughts of him from my mind. I looked forward to meeting him again soon.

Zach

Tools were everywhere. Repairs and renovations had just begun, and I was already done with it all. Every contractor had some sort of problem today that I had to deal with. I was beyond exhausted and had never been so happy to see a day end as I was today. I'd just shut and locked the front door and was on my way into the kitchen when Grace came flying down the stairs, cell phone in hand. It hadn't been my idea to give an eleven-year-old a cell phone. It had been her mother's. Valerie had done many things I wasn't happy with this past summer, but that one was the icing on the cake.

"I told you, I don't want you spending time on that thing," I called.

She completely ignored me, heading toward the kitchen. I followed behind her and stepped into the kitchen, only to find her digging through the cupboard where I kept all her snacks.

"What are you doing now?" I demanded.

"Getting a snack," she muttered with her head in the cupboard.

"It's almost time for dinner. You don't need a snack," I replied, waiting for her to pop her head out of the cupboard. When she did, I snatched her cell phone from her hand.

"Dad!"

"Grace, I told you. I don't want you on that thing. Now, you must have some homework to do."

She looked up at me with tears in her eyes and took off for the stairs. "I'm calling Mom."

"Go ahead!" I yelled just as my mother came into the kitchen.

"Everything okay?" she asked.

"Fine," I barked.

We both looked toward the hall as Grace stomped up the stairs as hard as she could, and then slammed her bedroom door shut, causing the plaster on the ceiling of the kitchen to fall onto the countertops. I gripped the edge of the counter and took a deep breath, trying hard to not lose my temper at the sight of one more thing that needed to be repaired.

"Well, I guess I will add the kitchen ceiling to the list of repairs," my mother said, grabbing a pen and the list of all the things that we needed to repair.

"I'm going to go upstairs and have a chat with little miss attitude," I grumbled, heading toward the bottom of the stairs when the phone rang.

"Zach, it's for you. It's one of the contractors!" my mother yelled.

I'd had it out with two contractors today and just didn't have the will to have another conversation with one of them or one with my daughter. Plus, I had a pile of things to do after Grace was in bed, so I turned around and made my way back into the kitchen and took the phone from my mother.

We'd eaten out the last three nights. I needed to make something homemade. After hanging up the phone, I scratched my head as I looked in the cupboards to see what there was for dinner and then went to the drawer where my mother had shoved a pile of easy to make recipes there. I sifted through them, finally deciding on chicken tacos.

The chicken was in the pan on the stove cooking away, while mom was cutting up the veggies and I grated the cheese. Everything was coming together quickly. I'd just placed all veggies on the table, along with the shells, and went to grab the chicken from the pan when the doorbell rang.

"Watch that," I said to my mom, shaking the pan of chicken, leaving it to cook a little longer.

I stepped into the hallway to see if I could see who was at the door but couldn't. I glanced back at the stove to see my mom watching over it. The second I opened the door, I wished I'd not bothered. Valerie stood there, looking less than pleased.

She shoved me out of the way and stepped into the house. I was just about to ask her what she was doing there when the fire alarm started going off. I took off toward the kitchen, which was now filled with smoke, to find my mom waving the towel under the smoke detector. I quickly removed the pan containing the chicken off the stove and grabbed the flipper I'd been using and pushed at the few burnt pieces, quickly adding a little water to help remove them from the bottom of the pan. Then I opened the window and shoved it open.

"I see nothing has changed here," Valerie said, placing her purse on the island in the kitchen and crossing her arms over her chest. "Mona," she bit out.

My mother dropped the towel on the island and looked at me. "I'll be in the other room."

I didn't blame my mother. She'd never been able to stand Valerie, and she'd told me after we'd split that when and if she came around, she would leave.

I ignored Valerie's comment and scooped the chicken into a bowl and then went to call for Grace, who surprised me by coming around the corner.

"Mom!" she screamed, running over, and wrapping her arms around Valerie. "What are you doing here?"

Valerie hugged Grace to her and then smiled down at her. "Who did your hair?" she questioned, running her hand over the messy ponytails.

"Dad. He isn't as good at them as you," she muttered, looking over at me. "He also took my phone."

I gripped the edge of the counter, praying that it stopped me from hitting something or someone, and I didn't mean Grace. I could tell from the look in Valerie's eyes that she was less than impressed.

"Why would you take her phone away?" she questioned, turning toward me.

"Valerie, an eleven-year-old does not need a phone. She doesn't need a device to text with other kids, or god only knows who."

"I gave it to her so she could get ahold of me whenever she wants."

I clenched my jaw tight. "That is why I pay every month for a phone and the internet. So she can call you when she wants. I've never denied her that."

"What about while she is at school?"

I dropped the bowl of chicken into the centre of the table and turned to face Valerie. "She does not need to contact you when she is at school. She is there to learn, not message her mother."

"Says you. What if she needs something and you aren't

around?"

I let out a deep breath and counted to five. "Where the hell would I be?"

"Who knows? You could be stuck in renovations or...I don't know, having coffee with some woman at the diner in town while your daughter is stuck waiting for a ride."

There it was. Grace had been upset when I'd picked her up last night because I'd been fifteen minutes late. It hadn't been a big deal; I hadn't been the only parent who'd been late. However, sometime between bedtime last night and today, Grace had divulged what I'd told her. That I'd been late because I'd been having coffee with a friend. I'd not mentioned it was a woman, but knowing Valerie, she had probably inserted that little tidbit on her own.

I glanced over to Grace, who sat at the table looking my way, a tight smile on her lips. God, she was just like her mother.

"Dinner is all burnt up," she cried, picking up a piece of chicken and throwing it on her plate.

Valerie looked over at me, a scowl on her face. "Is that what you're calling dinner?" she questioned, walking over to the table, routing through the bowl of chicken, picking up a burnt piece between her fingers and scowling.

"Yes, that is dinner. There is nothing wrong with it. It got a little overcooked because I had someone unexpected show up at the door."

"Gracie, why don't you go upstairs and get changed? Mom will take you out for something."

"She isn't going out for food. Now, Grace, head up to your room. Give me a few minutes to make more chicken and get your mother out of here and on her way, and we will sit down and eat."

Grace looked between her mother and me and then let out a huff. "I want to go out." She scowled, crossing her arms.

I was at the end of my rope. It had been clear why the courts had given me full custody of Grace. Valerie couldn't hold down a job, had men coming and going all hours of the night, allowed Grace to do whatever she wanted, and she had little to no set rules for her to follow. Leaving her for the few weeks during the summer had probably been a huge mistake on my part, and one I would pay for, for months to come.

"I told you to go to your room. Give me a few minutes."

I bent down and reached into the snack cupboard, producing a chocolate bar I'd hidden, and held it up for Grace to take, which she did with a smile and disappeared. I listened as I heard her climb the stairs and then shut her bedroom door. Then I turned to Valerie.

"Care to tell me what it is you are doing here?" I questioned.

Valerie glanced around the kitchen and then met my

eyes. "I need some money," she whispered, glancing over to the room my mother was in.

I looked over at the woman whose hair was perfectly styled and never went a month without a colour touchup. She wore a designer suit and had the latest Louis Vuitton shoes on her feet. She even carried one of their top bags over her arm. "You need money?" I questioned; not sure I heard her right.

She nodded. "Some things have come up."

I wasn't sure what to say. I looked around the at thousands of dollars in materials I'd had to purchase for this renovation and wondered if she'd lost her damn mind. I was the one who was responsible for Grace and making sure she had a roof over her head. I had no responsibility to pay this woman. The judge hadn't even forced her to pay child support since I'd been the sole provider to the family. I was damn lucky that my lawyer fought to get me out of paying for her comfortable lifestyle.

I cleared my throat. "Please tell me you are kidding."

"No, I need some money."

"I'm sorry there, but the bank of Zach is closed. It closed the day you bedded the nineteen-year-old neighbour, remember."

"Zach, please. This is important."

"So were lawyers' fees, but somehow you scraped those up while going behind my back and trotting around town with that boy toy of yours. Why don't you go ask him for some money?"

Valerie looked at me, a funny look on her face. She swallowed hard and shoved her hands in her pockets. "Don't be ridiculous. He doesn't have any money."

"I'm being ridiculous? The only one who was ridiculous was you, leaving me for him. Now, I said it before, and I'll say it again. I think you need to have your head checked."

"Does that mean you will not help me out?"

I chuckled under my breath before growing serious. "That, my dear, is exactly what it means. You'll have to find the next fool who will cover your expenses. Now, I need to get dinner on," I said, turning and pulling out another frozen package of chicken and throwing it in the microwave to thaw it.

The room was silent, and when I turned around, Valerie stood there looking at me. "Please, Zach, would you reconsider?"

I just shook my head. I grabbed her purse from where she'd left it on the counter and shoved it into her hand. "You've got to go," I said, turning her around and leading her to the front door. I didn't give her time to protest. Instead, I opened the door, ushered her out, and then locked the door behind her and made my way back into the kitchen where I took a bit and cooked the chicken again, this time not burning it.

Iris

"I had Thomas set up the backyard with some picnic tables and chairs for today's story time," Trinity said, coming out of the kitchen and into the store. "I think it will be nice for you and the kids to sit out back today. It's beautiful out there."

I smiled and nodded. "Yes, it's one of the nicer days we've had lately. I spent so much time inside during the summer organizing the house that I want to soak up as much of the sunshine as I can before winter."

"Thomas is trying to get another permit for an extension on this building, but the town is giving us trouble. He said if worse comes to worse, he'll build a room under his workshop for us to use during the winter."

I hadn't even thought about winter and what that

would mean for the reading program, since we only started it a few weeks earlier.

"I fear I'm just outgrowing this space for all I want to do," Trinity said, grabbing a pile of books from a box and heading toward the shelves to place them.

"Would you consider moving if need be?"

Trinity shook her head. "No, if you remember, this was my aunt's bookstore before mine. I'd never give it up." She smiled.

"Maybe we could clean out one of the storage areas in the back there as an option."

Trinity thought for a moment and nodded. "Could work. Then I could use the area under Thomas's workshop as storage. You might be onto something there."

Just then, the door opened and in walked three kids. "Hi, Iris. We are here for story time."

"I guess that is my cue." I smiled, reaching for the book I'd chosen for today's story hour, along with my coffee.

"Don't forget the snacks in the kitchen," Trinity called.

I rushed around and then made my way back out front where more kids had gathered with Trinity. She showed them to the back door and led them out into the yard while I grabbed one more book from the counter. I was just about to head out when the bells jingled above the door, and I turned to see Zach standing there holding a copy of the book I'd be reading today.

"Are you returning that book late as well?" I smiled.

He chuckled and placed the book under his arm. "No, I just thought I'd come by with Grace and offer my support. She wanted to listen to you read," he said, nodding toward the truck where I saw Grace climbing out.

"Iris, they are all set up out back," Trinity said, coming around the corner and sitting down behind the desk.

"We have one more straggler." Zach chuckled and opened the door in time for Grace, who wore a sour face, to step inside. She carried a few books in her arms and came over beside him.

"Can we please get started?" she grumbled.

I looked at Zach and smiled. There was no doubt she was his child. She looked exactly like him.

"I'm Iris," I said, coming down to her eye level.

"Grace." She held out her tiny hand.

"What do you say we head out back? There are a bunch of other kids out there too, my son included."

She flipped her hair over her shoulder and walked beside me to the backyard, where she took a seat beside her father.

Every child listened with intent as I read three chapters from the first book in *The Baby-Sitters Club* books. Once I finished, we talked about what we'd read and then I handed out the snacks and let the kids talk. I made my way over to where Zach stood.

"How did you enjoy that?" I questioned.

"I'm not really a *Baby-Sitters Club* fan, but I didn't find it too bad." Zach chuckled.

I smiled. "Think the kids enjoyed it?"

"I do. I think it's a great program to be honest. It's gotten Grace to read as you can see," Zach said, nodding toward Grace, who sat there with a pile of books in front of her. "I'm also hoping that she will make some new friends through the program. She's been pretty upset since moving here. She's away from all her friends."

I nodded. "I get that. Noah and Dylan have been the same. It's been hard on them as well. I worry. They pulled into themselves once they lost their father. They pulled away from their friends, and I took them away from them when they finally came back out of their shell."

"Don't be so hard on yourself. It was a traumatic time for, not only them, but you as well. Sometimes, we have to do what is best for ourselves, not only what's best for them," Zach said, nodding toward Grace.

I looked over and noticed Noah tapping her on the shoulder. I smiled when she turned around and began talking a mile a minute to him, showing him the books in her pile.

"I know. Don't you feel bad?"

Zach shrugged. "Sure. However, to save my daughter from becoming her mother, it had to be done."

"Oh dear. That sounds like a story for another time."

"Probably best." He winked.

I glanced at my watch and noticed it was almost time for the kids to be picked up. "Excuse me for a moment," I said, stepping away from where we'd been standing and making my way over to where I'd been sitting. "Alright, kids. Listen, your parents will be here shortly. Now is the time to hit the store and check out the reading library to see what you'd like to borrow until next time. Gather any books you need to return and any of your belongings and follow me."

I watched as the kids gathered up their things and formed a line behind me. Then we all headed back into the store. The kids went right over to the dedicated shelves, and the ones with books to return got in line. I quickly began processing them as some parents arrived to gather their kids.

It took about twenty minutes before I got everyone processed and sent the last group of kids home. Suddenly, a pile of books slammed down on the lower part of the counter. I glanced over and spotted Grace standing there, her arms crossed, tapping her foot on the ground. I glanced up at Zach, who shrugged and winked at me.

"Hi, Grace. Did you need to return these?"

"Yes. I've only been waiting for like ever."

"Well, I'm sorry. I didn't see you. Now, did you want to take any more books home with you?"

"Yes, but Dad said I can only have three."

I glanced up at Zach, who shook his head, telling me he had said nothing of the sort. I smiled. "Alright, well, three is still a good number of books. So, let's get these checked in and those checked out, okay?"

Once I had finished, I got up and came around the counter. "Have a good night, Grace."

She continued to the door and went to push it open when Zach stopped her. "What do you say, Grace?"

"Thanks, Iris. See you next week."

"See you, Grace. Enjoy those books, okay?"

Grace stopped walking and turned toward Zach. "Are you coming, Dad? We don't have all day," she said, putting her hand on her hip.

I tried hard not to laugh.

"I'll be right there. Go climb in the truck," Zach said, then glanced over at me and smiled.

Zach and I watched as Grace made her way over to his truck. "Sorry about that. She's got..."

"Spunk?" I asked.

"Attitude. I was going to say. Just like her mother."

I laughed. "Yeah, that she does have." I winked. "It's not much different from my two, to be honest. I'm sure she will outgrow that."

Zach stood there, shifting from foot to foot. Clearly, he wanted to say something.

"Well, it was nice to see you again. I guess I will see you next week at the next reading." I smiled, stepping away and heading back toward the desk. When I sat down, I noticed he was still standing there, fidgeting. "Is there something else?" I questioned.

He glanced over to where Trinity stood speaking with another customer before making his way over to me, then leaned on the counter. "I thought maybe we could get lunch or coffee sometime, if you aren't too busy, but I totally understand if you are, because well, just because I do," he said quietly.

I smiled again and looked down at the counter, my cheeks getting a little hot at his question. Just then the bells above the door chimed and in walked Carol and her daughter, Mizzy. Carol glanced between the pair of us and gave us a nod, then made her way over to where Trinity stood with Peggy. Their mumbled words were barely audible as they talked amongst themselves while looking over at Zach and me.

"If you aren't interested...just forget that I asked. I think I may have overstepped my bounds," he said, placing his hand on the door and pushing it open.

"Wait, one minute," I said, coming back around the counter and making my way over toward Zach. We both stepped outside, the fresh air welcoming. Immediately, I spotted Grace staring at us through the truck window, a tiny frown on her face.

I shoved a folded piece of paper into his hand and met his eyes. "My number. I think dinner sometime would be wonderful, and I'd love to have a coffee afterward," I said, smiling up at him.

Zach nodded and lifted his eyes to mine. "I like food with coffee." He winked.

"Okay."

"Alright. I'll see you soon."

"See you soon."

I watched as Zach headed toward his truck and climbed in. Within seconds, the engine fired up, and the truck pulled away from the curb. I jumped when I felt someone pull on my arm.

"Mom...can we please go home?" Noah said, looking up at me. "Dylan and I want to watch our show and it's on soon."

I turned my attention to my boys, who now stood beside me, and smiled. "Of course. Let's get our things and get going."

I made my way back into the store, while Dylan and Noah went to the car. The instant I stepped inside, Trinity and Peggy questioned me.

"What was that all about?" Trinity asked, a knowing smile on her face.

"Oh nothing," I answered, my cheeks heating.

"It didn't look like nothing." Peggy smiled. "It looked like perhaps he may have asked you on a date."

"No, his um...his daughter Grace, she needs help with

reading, and he asked if I could possibly come over and give her a hand."

Trinity shook her head. "So full of denial. He's a looker. Enjoy your date."

A smile fell to my lips as I reached behind the counter and grabbed my purse. "You two are impossible," I said as I headed to the door.

"Not impossible, just nosey." Peggy laughed.

"See you both soon. Have a good day."

The rest of the week flew by. I'd had no more problems with contractors or with Grace. In fact, things were going so well, I wondered what the next bomb would be to drop. I sat in the kitchen, sunlight coming through the window, enjoying my morning coffee while my mother and I looked at tile choices for the bathroom that Alexa had picked for us. I slid one across to the pending pile and was sipping my coffee when Grace came flying into the kitchen.

"Morning," she sang.

"Morning," we muttered, trying to decide between two options that both worked well with the floor tile.

"What are you doing?" she asked, climbing up on the stool of the breakfast bar.

"Choosing tile for the bathrooms," I grunted. I was

not good at this part. Valerie hadn't been wrong about that when we were married, and it was showing. I shoved the tiles away from me. "Perhaps we should just have Alexa choose," I said to my mother.

Alexa had come highly recommended from two businesses in the area, so my mother hired her almost on the spot, and I'd never been more grateful, especially the deeper into the project we got.

"Grace, what would you like to do today?" I asked.

I'd been trying to keep her occupied on Sundays. It was the one day of the week I didn't have contractors pouring through the house and one day that we could just spend some father-daughter time without interruption.

"Can we go out for dinner?"

I shrugged. "Sure. You tired of my home-cooked meals?"

"You aren't that great of a cook, Dad," she said, making a face that made me laugh inside.

"Alright, well, where would you like to go?"

She brought her finger up to her lips and lifted her eyes, looking at the ceiling, thinking hard. "Ummmm...how about that family restaurant we passed the one day a few weeks ago?"

I frowned, wondering what restaurant she meant. We'd driven in and out of Willow Valley many times in the past few weeks, not to mention throughout the town many times. "Hmmm, which place?"

"The Lounge place," Grace said, giving me a serious look, as if I should know exactly where she was talking about.

"Gracie, I don't know where you mean. Can you tell me where we were going when we passed it?"

"To the city, Dad."

I ran through what I could remember, still coming up with nothing. Then Grace ran out of the room and upstairs, finally coming back down only a few minutes later, holding her phone.

"This place," she said, holding her phone up for me to see.

"Oh, The Cedar Grill and Lounge?" I frowned, wondering why she had chosen that place out of them all. "I guess we can go there."

"Yay!" Grace said, jumping up and down in excitement.

I shook my head and pulled the tiles back in front of me, while Grace climbed back up on the stool. Before I got too invested in the project at hand, I poured her a bowl of cereal, and while she ate, I tried once again to pick the tiles for the bathrooms.

My day was full of laundry. Grace helped me around the house with a few chores, and before I knew it, it was time to climb into the car and head to the restaurant. I'd just pulled off the road into the restaurant parking lot, found a spot, and parked the car. I glanced into the rearview mirror in time to see Grace give me an odd smile.

"What's that look for?" I questioned.

"Nothing, Daddy. I'm just so excited that we can have dinner as a family."

"We have dinner as a family all the time, Gracie," I muttered, pulling my keys from the ignition, wondering what the hell she meant by that.

She shook her head. "No, it's been a while, Daddy."

I shook my head and climbed out of the car and made my way around to the back passenger's side, wondering what on earth Gracie was mumbling about. I was about to open the door when I heard a familiar voice behind me.

"It's about time you got here. I've been waiting for over twenty minutes."

I was certain the blood drained from my face as I whipped around to see Valerie standing there. How had I been wrangled into some weird web of deception by my eleven-year-old daughter to have dinner with her mother?

"What are you doing here?" I muttered.

"Having dinner, as a family."

Before she could continue, I held up my hand and shook my head. "Never mind. I don't want to hear it."

I returned to the table and sat down in the far corner of the booth opposite Valerie. Grace sat beside her mother, looking at the menu with her, nodding away as Valerie spoke to her and pointed things out.

I had nothing to say to her at all. I'd already decided that Grace was going to be grounded before we got home, and that the cell phone was going in the garbage. Glancing down at the menu, trying to diffuse my anger at the situation, I ran my fingers through my hair and looked at the menu, finally settling on wings and fries.

Grace was chatting away when I put the menu down and noticed Valerie was staring at me. I frowned and mouthed, "What?" but she just sat there, still giving me a dirty look.

Was this because I hadn't yet agreed to give her the money? If it was, she'd be giving me that look for a long while yet, because there was no way in hell I was going to buckle. If anything, Valerie owed me the money for the last year and a half of supporting Gracie. Not that I'd ever ask, because I didn't need it, and it gave me pleasure to pay for all the things she needed. If only I'd known what I was getting myself into with Valerie when I'd met her, I never would have ever gotten involved. However, I wouldn't have Grace then either.

I'd never have denied her money either, except for when she went for a younger version of me. It all went downhill for her after that. She soon lost her job and hadn't been able to keep one since. What money she earned and had saved went to partying with her friends and lavish trips, along with the same expensive clothes I used to provide her with. It wasn't my problem. She was broke and there was no way in hell she was going to make me believe it was my problem so that I'd fix it.

When it came time to order, I could barely get a word in edgewise. Instead, Valerie ordered for all of us. I frowned as I watched her decide, choosing dishes I knew Grace would never touch. As she continued, I looked down at the menu, adding up every item she'd asked for. Yep, just like her, I thought to myself as the bill was easily hitting the one-hundred-dollar mark.

Just like I thought, neither Grace nor I touched dinner once it arrived. Valerie ordered nothing we liked, and she questioned me about it as the server was clearing the table.

"The food was good. I don't know why neither of you ate."

"Because, Mom, it looked all slimy, especially the green stuff," Grace said, looking over at me with a disgusted expression on her face.

"That was creamed spinach, Grace. It's so good for you. Much better than some of the stuff you've been eating lately."

Valerie loved to make a scene and would do anything for an audience. I knew Grace was starving, so I asked the server to bring over an ice cream sundae and watched with a smile as Grace dug her spoon into the chocolaty mess.

"Grace shouldn't have all that sugar, Zach. Is that what you feed her, because she barely touched any of her dinner," Valerie said, digging in her purse and pulling out a gold-plated compact and blotted her nose with powder.

"Yeah, well, she certainly would not touch the creamed spinach, and as for the rest of the items you chose, they left much to be desired. Plus, you know she's a picky eater, and I will not force her to eat something she doesn't like," I said, my jaw tight as I picked up the bill from the table and looked at the total.

"Oh, so you feed her nothing but sugar. It's not a wonder why she flies around all the time like she's on some sort of sugar high," Valerie said, taking the spoon from Grace's hand and placing it down on the table.

Grace looked at me, clearly upset at the fact that Valerie had ripped the spoon away from her.

"God, Valerie, I don't," I said through clenched teeth. "If you would have let me just order, she'd have eaten her damn dinner," I said, slamming the bill down harder on the table than I'd intended.

Grace jumped and looked at me and then at her mother. As soon as Valerie took her eyes off Grace, she picked up the spoon and dug it back into the ice cream.

"Zach, really, you need to work on your temper," Valerie said, leaning toward me so she could keep her voice low. She then turned back to Grace and took the spoon from her hand again, this time setting it on the opposite side of her.

"No more sugar. Dammit, Grace, you should have just eaten your dinner," Valerie said, roughly wiping the mixture of ice-cream and chocolate off her face.

"The only thing I need to work on is keeping you away from me. You are the only temper causing issue in my life. Let the child eat," I said, placing the spoon back in front of Grace.

"She doesn't need all that sugar," she said, pulling the spoon away from her. "Anyway, I think it's time to end this night right here." Valerie pushed the bowl away from Grace. She then went to pull her to her side, but Grace shoved at her.

"I want Dad!" she screamed, causing people to look in our direction.

I stood up and waited for Valerie to move. When she did, I held out my hand for Grace to take while she continued to cry. I turned and headed toward the door and put Grace in the truck. Minutes later, I returned to the restaurant to our table. I slid into the booth across from Valerie and looked at her.

"What did you do with Grace?" she questioned.

"What do you think I did with her? I put her in the truck. Now, let's get a few things straight before we go."

Valerie sat back, a look of shock on her face as she

waited for me to speak. It was rare I spoke to her in this tone, but I'd had enough.

I grabbed the bill and held onto it. "Now, there is no way on earth I am giving you the money you want. So, let's get that straight. Second, no more showing up unannounced. If you want to see Grace, I ask for at least a week's notice, which is less than the court determined was fair. If you make it any more difficult than saying yes, I have no problem heading back to my lawyer."

Valerie brought her hand up to her chest. "Zach...I don't...understand."

"Let's drop the innocence act here. You are a damn mess. Everyone can see it but you. Get your shit together and do it fast."

I slid from the booth and made my way to the counter to pay the tab. Then, without looking back, I headed to the truck and took Gracie home.

I rubbed my eyes and shut my laptop down. I never thought I'd be back to late night hours, but here I was. At least this was my choice and not the boss telling me I had a deadline to hit.

I stretched and looked down at my phone to see a message waiting. I opened the screen and smiled as I saw Iris's name.

We'd been messaging on and off since Friday afternoon. She'd needed some help to fix a couple of small things, and I'd been more than happy to help her.

Zach: Sorry I was out at dinner when you messaged.

Iris: No worries. I just wanted to let you know I got the door repaired.

Zach: Good stuff. I knew you could do it. It wasn't that hard.

Iris: Nope, not hard at all, just took me and the two boys to get it done. Getting them to listen to instructions was the hard part. It was an adventure.

Zach: I told you if you needed me, I'd come over. You should have just asked.

Iris: Is that you offering? Because I may still need you. The tap in the bathroom needs replacing and, well, I know nothing about plumbing. I tried to watch some YouTube videos, but I'm still lost.

Zach: No problem, I can pop over in the morning.

Iris: Great, oh I did manage to purchase a tap at the hardware store tonight.

Zach: Perfect. I'll see you about ten?

Iris: Ten works. See you then.

The next morning, I dropped Grace off at school, swung over to The Crispy Biscuit, and then made my way over to the address Iris gave me. I walked up to the door and knocked.

I waited a few minutes and knocked again. This time the door flew open, and Iris stood there, her white T-shirt soaked through giving me quite the view. Her hair was everywhere, and she looked completely frazzled.

"Come in, come in," she said, frantically rushing back into the house.

"If I had known we were having a wet T-shirt contest here, I'd have come better prepared," I said as I stepped inside and shut the door behind me and poked my head into the kitchen to see her holding a towel around the tap, which was spraying water all over the kitchen. I quickly put down the coffee I'd brought and ran over to her, dropping to the floor. Reaching under the sink, I shut off the water and stood up.

"Thank goodness you arrived when you did," Iris said, now letting go of the towel. "You are a hero!"

"What happened?" I questioned, trying hard not to laugh.

Iris giggled. "I don't know. I turned the water on to fill the sink, and suddenly I was being sprayed in the face. Then there was water everywhere. You got here just in time. You saved me from a flood."

I looked down at the small puddle of water I was standing in and smiled. "Well, at least a bigger flood," I answered. "I brought coffee. How about we quickly soak up this water and then take a rest?"

"Oh, you really are a hero," she said, throwing her arms around my neck. I could feel my shirt getting soaked from hers. "Honestly, I haven't stopped this morning." She stepped back and looked down at my shirt, which was now wet as well. "Whoops, it appears I got you wet."

"Hey, that is supposed to be my line." I winked, watching as her cheeks turned pink.

"Yeah, well, I beat you to it." She giggled, now embarrassed, as she looked down at the front of her shirt to see it clinging to her skin. "I better change and get some towels."

Within minutes, Iris stood with a couple of dry towels in her hand, which we used to pick up the water while she rambled on about her morning and how the boys had refused to cooperate.

Once we finished, she looked up at me with a hint of a smile. "Thank you."

"You are welcome. Now, come on over and take a seat," I said, placing my hand on her lower back and guiding her over to the table where we sat and shared a coffee before getting to work on the faucet repairs.

I stirred the cheese packet into the macaroni on the stove and quickly flipped the hotdogs that were cooking away on the griddle. My stomach flipped as I added the milk and stirred. My nerves were getting the best of me.

After Zach had helped me fix the taps in the house, he stuck around and helped me with a few other things that needed more than one adult. Once we finished, I apologized again for the wet shirt and the view I'd given him. He smiled and told me I had nothing to worry about, and then he asked if I'd like to have dinner with him tonight.

Honestly, I couldn't wait for an evening with another adult, even if I was still embarrassed that he'd witnessed the wet T-shirt mess.

"Mom, why do we need a babysitter?" Dylan muttered from where he sat at the table doing his math homework.

"Well, because I'm going out and I'm not sure how late I will be. Leaving you alone for a few minutes after school is fine, but I can't leave you in charge of your brother for an entire evening. Besides, you like Ava."

I'd asked Ava if she'd mind staying with the boys tonight when I stopped in the bookstore this afternoon. She'd jumped at the chance. She'd been helping me with the reading program so she could get some volunteer credit hours for school and had taken a real liking to Noah and Dylan.

"She's alright I guess," Dylan said, putting his pencil down and picking up his eraser.

I smiled to myself. "You know, she may even help you with your homework. If you ask her nicely, that is."

Dylan shrugged and picked his pencil back up, putting it into his mouth while thinking through the problem. He'd been struggling with math, which was the subject his father used to help him with.

"Is dinner just about ready? I'm starved," Noah said, coming in the door and throwing his ball glove in the chair. He'd been out playing with some kids at the park and had walked through the door looking just like his father used to. It brought back a memory I wasn't prepared for at the moment. I saw more and more of Lucas in these boys every day. The older they got, the more I knew I'd see.

"Where are you going again?" Dylan questioned,

shoving his brother into the wall when they both went for the fridge door at the same time.

I stopped stirring the mac and cheese and froze. I hadn't told the boys that I was going on a date. In fact, I'd not mentioned Zach at all to them. I'd simply said I had gone for coffee with a friend the other night. "Just going out with a friend," I replied.

My stomach flipped again as the words fell from my mouth. I hated not telling the boys the full truth, and I'd flip if they lied to me or omitted things, and here I was doing the same thing.

"What time is Ava coming?" Noah asked, sitting down.

"She should be here soon," I said, quickly pouring the mac and cheese into the bowl and adding two hot dogs for each of the boys. "Here we go." I placed the bowls down on the table. "Oh, I forgot, these are for dessert..." I placed a box that contained three donuts from The Crispy Biscuit in the centre of the table.

"Thanks, Mom," Dylan said, digging into the creamy mixture.

"You can have them with Ava tonight while you are watching TV."

"You never let us have mac and cheese or hotdogs," Noah said.

"Or donuts," Dylan added.

Truth was, I wasn't in the mood to fight with them

tonight. I didn't want to have a war on my hands as I walked out the door, so an easy dinner I knew they loved was the right choice. "It's a treat. So, you boys enjoy. If you need me, I'll be upstairs."

I climbed the stairs quickly and headed into my bedroom, pulling the closet door open. Flipping through the dresses that hung there, I worried. I hadn't been on a first date in thirteen years. I did not know what people were even wearing on them anymore.

I shut the door to my bedroom and grabbed my cell phone, dialling my sister.

"What's up?" she asked breathlessly into the phone.

"Beth, I need help."

"What is it? Is it one of the boys?" she questioned concern filling her voice.

Did I sound that frantic? I thought I sounded calm, I thought to myself. "No, the boys are fine. I have a date tonight, and I don't know what to wear," I whispered, swallowing hard. Truth was I was trying to swallow down the butterflies that had been swirling in my stomach the entire afternoon and this evening. "As a matter of fact, I'm regretting even saying yes to this," I added, after thinking about yesterday morning and the fool I'd made of myself, opening the door, not thinking about how wet my shirt had been.

"WHAT?" The noise in the background stopped, and instantly I knew I'd caught my sister in the middle of her workout. "Now, you better spill it all and do it now."

"I don't have time to tell you about it now. I need you to tell me what on earth I should wear. You were the one who organized my closet," I mumbled, going back through them again. "You know what I have, so please, help me."

"Iris, I need details. What does said date look like? What on earth is so great about him that made you say yes? Lord knows I've tried to set you up with many eligible bachelors, all of which you didn't bother to contact again, may I add. I need these details in order to make my choice."

"Beth, come on, please. Which dress should I wear?"

Beth let out a sigh. "You'll probably hate me for this, so I am going to make you promise me you won't kill me first."

"What...fine...I promise."

"Reach into the back of your closet, left-hand side, and grab the last hanger."

"What did you do?" I questioned.

She let out a sigh. "You are so stubborn. Just do it."

I did what she told me, and what I removed stunned me. There in my hand was a beautiful beige dress. I could remember from the feel of the lightweight material that it felt amazing against my skin. It also hugged me in all the right places, and it had been something my sister had been dying to get me into for months and months. If I remembered correctly, she'd been angry at me when I'd refused to buy it. "Where did this come from?"

"A little mouse left it for you. EEEEK! A date finally!" Beth screamed into the phone.

"Is this the same dress you tried to get me to buy six months ago when we went on the girls' weekend?"

"Maybe..."

I looked at the dress that hung on the hanger, debating if I should just tuck it back in the closet again. It was a little much for a first date, at least in my mind and Beth would never know I didn't wear it.

"Don't you dare hang it back in that closet!"

I glanced around the room, looking to see if she'd installed cameras in here. How else could she have known that I was debating hanging it back where it belonged? I let out a deep breath and placed the dress on the bed.

"Now, tell me all about him."

"He just moved here. He is redoing the Willow Valley Bed and Breakfast."

"Oh, Harry and Bessy's old place. I was sad to hear about Harry. What is his name?"

"Zach."

"How did you meet?"

God, I felt as if I were in the middle of an inquisition. I reached for my brush and ran it through my hair. "It was odd, actually. He came into the bookstore to return a children's book."

Immediately, Beth began choking on whatever she was drinking. When she finally stopped coughing, she cleared her throat. "Childrens book? Dare I ask you if you are robbing the cradle?"

"Oh for the love of...no, he was returning a book for his daughter. Anyway, it didn't start out all peaches and cream, but we have since mended that."

"I see. A single dad, eh? Is he cute?"

"I think so," I answered, slipping out of my jeans, thinking of how sexy the man truly was.

"Okay, well, you better fill me in on all the details. Is he taking you somewhere nice?"

"A little place called The Italian Affair. Hold on."

I threw the phone down and quickly grabbed the dress that lay on the bed and slipped it over my head. The fabric was light but heavy enough that it slid down my body and hung exactly how I'd remembered. I glanced in the mirror at myself, running my hands down my sides. Then I reached for the phone.

"Now, you say he is a single dad. Do you know how he got rid of his ex-wife?" she questioned.

I cleared my throat. "No, why?"

"Just wondering."

"Beth?" I questioned, knowing full well she knew many people who lived up by the Willow Valley Bed and

Breakfast. In fact, one of her best friends lived there, and they spoke almost daily. She was also an avid murder mystery and thriller fan, so her imagination always ran overtime, and I could only imagine she was thinking of a plot in one of them.

"Well, it's just I was speaking with LuAnn not that long ago, and she mentioned that a woman arrived outside of the bed and breakfast the other night. She was outside watering her plants and could hear yelling. I'm just worried. What if this Zach is hiding some dirty secrets?"

I blew out the breath I was holding. LuAnn Billings worked for the Willow Valley Gazette. Ever since returning to the small town, I'd learned rather quickly who to keep away from, and she was one of them.

I just wished Beth would agree with that statement; however, they'd been friends since high school, so there was no telling her any different. Plus, she lived almost two hours away from here, so she'd never believe a lot of the things that were circulating in town about LuAnn. She also didn't know the damage that woman had done to many of the residents here.

"I'm sure he isn't hiding anything."

At the moment, shrugging it off was what I had to do. I wasn't sure I wanted to get in the middle of a bad separation. I wasn't sure I could handle anything like that for a first relationship, and if I were going to bring my boys into this, I wanted to make sure that things were stable for them, including any relationship I entered.

"Maybe I will just cancel," I muttered, sitting down on the end of the bed and looking at myself in the mirror.

"Nonsense. It's only a first date. You aren't marrying the guy. Go have fun. Call me when you are back."

"Alright, I have to go. Talk soon."

Fixing my hair and makeup one more time, I slipped my feet into my shoes and made my way down the stairs. I could already hear Ava in the kitchen talking with the boys.

I popped my head around the corner and glanced into the kitchen to see Dylan, Noah, and Ava sitting around the table. A bag of chocolate chip cookies sat beside the box of donuts, and each one of them was eating cookies. The three of them were talking and laughing, so I let them be. I wasn't sure I wanted to be around the boys now, what with the nervousness I was feeling. They were normally perceptive.

I walked into the living room and laid my clutch purse on the side of the chair, along with a light sweater. Then I glanced out the window. The street was dark.

I was about to head into the kitchen when the phone rang. "Hello," I answered.

"Iris, it's your mother. How's everything going?"

"Good, Mom. How's Dad doing?"

"He's just finishing out in the garden. You know your

father and his plants. So, what is this I hear that you have a date tonight?"

It was just like Mom jumping right to the point of why she called. No doubt Beth had called her right after we'd gotten off the phone and dished everything I'd told her. Now Mom had to find out for herself.

"It's just dinner with a friend."

"No way, no way are you going to try that. Beth told me all about it. She also told me all about the woman who was at his place the other night. The one that LuAnn told her about."

I took a deep breath and pinched the bridge of my nose. My nerves were bad enough about tonight. I didn't need my mother filling my head with all this stuff as well.

It was then I caught sight of myself in the mirror that hung in the living room. I'd overdressed, and I needed to go back up and change.

"Mom, I am sure it was nothing," I said, more to comfort myself than to calm my mother down.

"Iris, I just don't know if you should get involved with a man whose life is clearly upside down. You are barely back on your own feet after everything that happened."

This was exactly my mother. She'd been on me to date for ages. She'd told me it wasn't normal for someone to take so long at my age to find a new spouse. I was certain she'd gotten that from some talk show host she watched. Now, here we were. I had a date, and she was trying to talk me out of it because she didn't like some information some gossip queen had passed on.

"Mom, you don't even know him," I whispered, so the boys didn't overhear. "I also don't know his story, so before we jump to any conclusions, I think it's best if we stop this conversation right now."

"Iris, I know enough."

"No, you know what LuAnn Billings has spread to Beth. Which from word in this town could be just a pile of stuff she made up on her own."

"Iris, please."

"Mom, tell me, why the change of heart? You have been on me to date for almost a year. So, tell me, why should I not go out with this man?"

"Iris, do you not think it's odd that a woman came to the bed and breakfast and that LuAnn could hear yelling and screaming? So much so she felt the need to tell your sister about it?"

I let out a breath. "Mom, LuAnn Billings is noted to be one of Willow Valley's largest gossip centres. I'm going to take that information with a grain of salt. It's not a secret that Zach has a past, just as I do. He has an eleven-year-old daughter, so somewhere in his life, I'm certain he has an ex-wife. He didn't have her on his own."

I could hear my mother take a sharp breath. "You know?"

"Yes, Mother, I know he had to have been in a relationship prior to asking me out for dinner. In fact, I'd have been more worried if he hadn't. I'm also not going to jump to conclusions," I said with my jaw clenched. The seed of doubt had been planted and watered, and now I wondered if not only I shouldn't change, but if I shouldn't just cancel as well.

"Iris, I wish you'd just listen."

"I am listening, Mother. I'm finally dating again. Now, I have to go, or I'm going to be late."

We said goodbye, and I hung up the phone, ran my hands over my dress, smoothing the fabric one more time.

I could already hear Ava in the kitchen talking with the boys. I popped my head in and said goodbye and made my way out to the car. Nerves fluttered through me as I started the engine and backed out of the driveway.

All the way to the restaurant, all I could hear in my mind was Beth talking about Zach's neighbour and the woman who had shown up. I also heard the voice of my mother. I really hoped that I wasn't making a mistake by accepting his invitation to dinner.

I climbed out of the hot shower and wrapped a towel around my waist. With the hand towel that lay on the counter, I wiped at the fogged-up mirror, my reflection finally coming into view. I didn't know why I was so nervous about tonight. It probably had a lot to do with the way I'd been feeling most of the week. My worst fear was that Iris would be another Valerie.

My sister told me I was being silly, that most women were not like Valerie in the slightest. However, it was what I'd known. We'd divorced two years ago, were separated for two before that, and I'd been ready to date for a while, but this irrational fear had kept me from even trying to meet someone. In fact, it had kept me from even attempting to let my guard down enough to even ask someone to go out with me for a simple coffee.

I'd conquered that mostly because I'd felt like an ass for being so short that day in the bookstore. However, the more I got to know Iris, the more I liked her, and after spending that one morning together at her place fixing things around her house, I somehow let my guard down completely. So, dinner was a big step for me and one I hoped wouldn't be a mistake.

I dried off, made my way into my bedroom, slid into my boxers and then my dress pants. Then I grabbed my phone from the dresser and dialled my sister. The phone rang and rang, and I was just about to hang up when she finally answered.

"You two stop the fighting now," Kristy growled into the phone.

"I'm not doing anything." I chuckled, knowing full well she was talking to her two kids. "How's things?"

"God, Zach, these two are going to be the death of me. Grant should be home soon, I hope. Then I can take a break, go out for a bit, and he can look after these two."

I chuckled. "Remember how the hell we used to fight? Probably drove Mom nuts. I'll have to ask her."

"Let me know what she says. I like to think our arguments kept her young." We both burst out laughing. "So, what's up? What's going on?"

I ran my fingers through my hair and picked up the can of shaving cream on the counter, quickly spraying a pile into my hand and rubbing it onto my cheeks. I placed my phone down on the counter and hit the speaker phone. "I did it."

"What did you do?" she questioned.

"I asked a woman out for dinner."

"OH MY GOD. Give me a second to sit down before I faint."

"Come on, Kristy, knock it off." I chuckled.

"Seriously though. I'm shocked. I never thought it would happen. I figured you'd be single forever."

"Well, it did…"

I took a deep breath, not sure I wanted to admit the next part. I really liked Iris.

"But…"

"I'm having some serious regrets over here. I called you to talk me down."

"What's got you all wigged out, big bro?"

"What doesn't? Did I tell you Valerie appeared for dinner the other night?"

"No. What happened?"

"What didn't? She wanted money, and I guess she figured the first time she asked, my answer wasn't what she wanted to hear, so she'd try again. I think she thought I'd bend and give it to her. Instead, her actions ended up upsetting Grace, and that pissed me off even more than I already was."

"I hate to break it to you, but that woman doesn't

deserve a dime. You'd be foolish to hand over anything to her."

I cleared my throat and began shaving. "I wouldn't bend, but I don't like the way she messes with Gracie's head. She conspired with her to make me think the dinner was Grace's idea, when in fact it was Valerie who'd suggested it to Grace."

"Don't get me all stirred up. I hated her ever since I met her. Knowing she messes with Grace makes me irate as hell, so I get that, Zach, I do. I'm just glad that you took Grace away with you and that she isn't living with her anymore."

"Same here. It's bad enough I left her for the time I did when Mom and I were buying this place. Thing is, Gracie thinks the woman is wonderful, until she shows her true self. It took me hours the other night to get her to calm down and fall asleep."

"I know, Zach. It was what I never liked about her; she was always hiding something. You'll have to forgive me, though. I'm confused because I don't know what dinner the other night has to do with dinner tonight?"

I smiled. This was my sister. She had been fighting for me to get back in the ring and date again. She'd been the one pushing and pushing so that I'd do it. "I don't know, I guess I'm just afraid that..."

"You're afraid that this woman will be another Valerie. It's a valid concern. However, you must give her a chance.

Don't go paint her with the same brush. Especially when you have gotten no reason to think that."

I walked into the bedroom and heard a tiny knock on the door. "Listen, I have to go," I muttered.

"Alright, just do yourself a favour, get Valerie out of your head and just put your focus on being the best dad out there. Also, have fun on your date," Kristy said. "Oh and don't do anything I wouldn't do!"

"Does Grant know the things you wouldn't do?" I chuckled.

"Yeah, I guess that doesn't work so much anymore, does it?" She giggled. "Have a good night. Give Grace a hug for us."

"Will do. Night, and thanks."

I hung up and threw my phone down on the bed and pulled the bedroom door open. Grace stood there, holding onto her favorite doll. "Hey, Daddy. Can I come in?"

"Of course."

I watched as she made her way over to my bed and climbed up on it. Then she stood up on the mattress. I took a couple of steps toward her, reaching out to make sure she didn't fall, when she surprised me by wrapping her arms around my neck.

"I love you, Daddy." She rested her head on my shoulder and didn't let go.

I pulled her against me and hugged her. "You know I'll

always be here for you, right? That I love you too and that you mean the world to me."

She nodded and then pulled away. She then sat down, cross-legged, on the mattress and gave me a once-over.

"Why are you dressed so nice, Daddy?"

I reached for the shirt I'd hung on the chair in my room and put it on, then turned to look at Grace, who sat there with questioning eyes.

"I'm going out to dinner with a friend tonight, so Grandma is going to watch you."

Grace was quiet for a moment. She sat there tracing over the pattern on my comforter with her finger and then turned her big brown eyes on me. "Are you going out with the lady from the bookstore?"

Instantly, I turned away from her. Was Valerie putting this information into Grace's head? I knew she was perceptive as hell and wondered if perhaps she'd overheard Valerie ask me if I'd been with a woman the day I was late to pick up Grace. I composed myself, and then nodded. "Yes, Grace, it is Iris. She seems like a nice lady, don't you think?"

Grace said nothing for a few moments, then nodded. "She's okay."

I gave myself a once-over in the mirror, dark dress pants and a white dress shirt in an Italian restaurant. I went over to my closet and pulled out a black dress shirt and quickly changed.

"That's better. You look handsome," Grace said, sliding off the bed.

I looked down at her and smiled. "Want to walk me to the door?" I questioned.

Grace grabbed my hand and pulled me out of my bedroom and down the stairs to the front door. Minutes later, she stood with my mother, both of them waving as I backed out of the driveway and turned in the direction toward the restaurant.

I watched her walk across the parking lot and the second she saw me, she smiled. She looked beautiful in the dress she wore, her hair falling over her left shoulder.

I leaned in for a quick hug and then placed my hand on her lower back and guided her into the restaurant. They seated us over in the corner, away from almost everyone, which just added a little more intimacy to this date.

I swallowed hard as I closed the menu, finally having decided what I was going to order. She did the same, then picked up her wineglass and took a sip.

"Okay, so before we get started. I have a question; one I hope isn't too private to ask."

"Shoot."

She fidgeted in her seat and then leaned across and whispered, "Are you sure? It is sort of personal."

I swallowed. "No problem. I'm a pretty open book."

She looked around, and once again leaned over the table toward me. "What was your relationship like with your ex-wife?"

The second the words were past her lips, I choked on my wine. I hadn't been expecting a question like that right off the bat.

"I'm sorry, I just thought I'd ask. I'm probably prying way too much. It's my sister and mother's fault. They were filling my head with many things before I left tonight. I'm sorry about that." She looked around the restaurant, no doubt trying to figure out how on earth she was going to recover from asking me this type of personal question.

I took a sip of water, clearing my throat, and reached across the table, taking her hand in mine. "Iris, don't worry. You haven't upset me. I just wasn't expecting you to ask me that. However, I really don't want to start off on the wrong foot. That is why I said I was an open book."

"Oh no, Zach, really, I shouldn't be prying like that," she said, her cheeks growing a little more red.

"You aren't. So, now my ex, well, things were great until they weren't. As is usually the case. It started mainly with petty arguments. Things couple always fight over: who was going to vacuum, who was going to unload the dishwasher and do laundry over the weekend. At first, we'd been able to laugh them off, and then things turned nasty.

"We got irritated with one another easily. She'd call names, I'd call them back. These petty, silly disagreements slowly morphed into larger, more serious arguments. Soon we found we were spending our Sundays fighting over finances and attacking one another instead.

"I worked a considerably stressful job—I was a CFO of a large financial corporation—the hours were long, the pay was amazing, but she loved to spend. I never said no. In fact, I encouraged it.

"One night she came home, I'd had a stressful day at work, and she carried with her two large bags from Louis Vuitton. In the blink of an eye, she'd spent nearly ten grand on things she clearly didn't need. Her closet was full of all kinds of bags from there that I'd gotten her over the course of the previous year. When I voiced my concern, she just laughed it off, but then broke down into tears, saying I didn't want to see her happy."

I picked up my wineglass and took a drink. "Shortly after that, she asked if I minded if she took a vacation with some friends of hers. Grace was about four, and with the hours I'd been working, the personal side of our relationship was beginning to suffer. I figured maybe it would do us good to have some time apart. So, I agreed and hired daycare for Grace for a week."

"What happened?" Iris questioned, eyes wide.

"Well, when she returned, so did the arguments. At the end of the summer, things were rocky at home. One afternoon, I came home and found Valerie crying in the living room. She claimed Grace was becoming too much for her to handle. She told me her doctors diagnosed her with a bout of depression, so to take the pressure off I put Grace into daycare at my office three days a week. Soon after when I'd come home with Grace at five, Valerie would be nowhere to be found.

"Over the coming weeks, this became a common occurrence. One evening I'd come home with Grace. We were in the middle of a huge audit at work, and I'd been told I had to return a couple of hours later. However, Valerie didn't come home that night, and I couldn't get ahold of our sitter, so I had to work from home. After Grace was in bed, I'd come down into the kitchen a few hours later to refill my coffee, and that was when I spotted Valerie. She was outside in our backyard in the hot tub with another man."

"What? Oh, Zach, I'm so sorry. What did you do?"

I shrugged. "What could I do? I was knee deep in reports for work that had a very short deadline, one that was closing in, so I said nothing. I didn't even confront them. When Valerie came home, she pretended nothing was up. I didn't want to acknowledge what was really going on, but soon I started having trouble at work, trouble concentrating, and I worried about Grace constantly when I left her with Valerie. So, I started taking Grace to work with me five days a week and placing her in daycare. A few weeks later, I hired a private investigator to follow Valerie. Our sex life, at this point, was so non-existent it was ridiculous, and she'd taken to sneaking out of the bedroom throughout the night. It wasn't long before the investigator confirmed what I already knew. She was cheating on me. I am not sure if that was the worst part, though."

Iris looked at me, confusion in her eyes. "The cheating wasn't the worst part?"

I shook my head. "No, it wasn't even the fact she'd meet with the guy every chance she got. The worst for me was that she was sleeping with a younger man. Our nineteen-year-old neighbour."

Iris's jaw dropped at my response.

"I gave everything to my lawyer. The divorce was nasty. I moved in with my sister for a bit afterward with Grace. Shortly after, I retired from my job. I'd done well for myself over the years and really couldn't take the stress of that lifestyle anymore. Of course, Valerie still comes around. I'd left Grace with her for a couple of weeks, while I came out to Willow Valley to look at the bed-and-breakfast with my mother. That had been a mistake. After

Grace was home, I didn't hear from Valerie for months. She's just recently resurfaced again and wants money."

"Wow, just wow. I'm so sorry that this is happening and happened to you."

I shrugged again and picked up my wine. "Whatever I did to piss off the guy upstairs, I'm hoping my punishment is almost over."

"Oh, Zach. You're not at fault for how she behaves. We have no control over other people's actions."

"This is true." I felt lighter knowing she knew the full truth now, and the fact she hadn't left the table said something as well.

"Just so you know I'm happy to listen anytime you need a shoulder."

"Thank you. Now, since we are on a sharing path, how about you tell me about your marriage and what happened?"

I watched as Iris picked up her glass and took a drink. The far-off look in her eyes, and the fact she hadn't started telling me, gave me cause for concern.

"If you'd prefer not to tell me, that is okay," I said, trying to reassure her I wasn't trying to impose.

"Oh, it's not that I won't talk about it. I'm just trying to figure out where to start. My relationship wasn't like yours. The opposite, in fact."

"I'm glad to hear that. Just start wherever you are comfortable."

"Lucas was my college sweetheart. We got married right after we graduated, and life began. We had Dylan and Noah. We were going to try for a girl when Noah was three, but Lucas started not to feel well.

"At first, he was just tired all the time. Then the headaches began. Debilitating headaches, so bad that when one would strike, I'd have to get him from work. He complained the lights were so bright they'd make him feel nauseous. Soon they began coming in droves. Stress seemed to cause them, so his doctor took him out of work, figuring it could be related to work stress.

"He was off for a couple of weeks, and things seemed to get better. The doctor kept him off another month, and by that time the headaches were much worse, lasting two to three days. One night he got up to clear the table after dinner and he passed out cold on the floor."

I swallowed hard and was glad for a break when our meal came.

We both dug into our dishes and closed our eyes at the same time. "God, this is good," Zach muttered.

"Yes, it is," Iris said, licking her lips while digging back into her dish.

"Alright, so you were saying. He'd passed out during dinner."

"Yes. I, of course, immediately called an ambulance. I'd been on Lucas to have his doctor run more tests, but he refused to ask. I think it probably scared him to investigate any more into the cause.

"Finally, we were in the hospital, and fortunately, he was put under the care of an excellent doctor who immediately began a myriad of tests. I sometimes wonder if knowing wasn't worse than not knowing after we found out that Lucas had a brain tumour."

I looked at Iris, who sat across from me with watery eyes. The last thing I wanted was for her to break down in tears. After all, this was our first night out together.

"Hey, if this is too much for you to talk about, then we can move on to something a little lighter," I whispered.

"No, just the memories are hard. Anyway, the doctor had put him on some medication for the headaches, and once they worked, I was hopeful everything would be okay. Of course, we had appointments with other doctors and such to discuss treatment options, and we were navigating those as best as we could.

"His first two scans showed zero signs of growth, and doctors were optimistic it wasn't cancerous. However, six months later, that was the one that read differently. The tumour had grown considerably, and, upon further investigation, he was diagnosed with brain cancer. Completely untreatable. They couldn't do anything. We were given a date, and we did what we could for the next year.

"We took the boys on day trips and took vacations

until Lucas could no longer get out of the house. Shortly before the end of that one year, a hospice worker moved into the house, and he passed away almost to the day of the date we'd been given. Noah was five, Dylan was seven, and here I was left with these two boys and no clue what I was going to do."

"Well, now that I've heard this, my problems seem to be nothing but silly."

Iris shook her head. "Don't be silly. We both lost something that we thought would last forever. It's difficult, no matter how it happens. I don't put weight on my story or yours. They are both equal in my mind. Some people would be destroyed if they lived either of our lives."

"This is true. So, what did you do?"

"Well, I had some help from my parents and my sister. We took the time we needed to adjust. This year, I sold the house we had and put that money into the house here. I grew up in Willow Valley, and even though it has changed, I wanted something like it for my boys to grow up in. I didn't want to worry about the influences of the other kids in the schools in the city, and I was afraid with what the boys had been through with their father that it would be easy for them to fall into a dangerous crowd."

"Makes sense. So you moved here."

"We did. The kids have finally started making friends and, for once, have smiles on their faces."

"Well, just like you, Iris, I can be a shoulder should you need anything. I can also help with the boys if you need."

"I'd appreciate that."

We grew quiet as we sat there eating the rest of our dinner. We ordered coffee and dessert, and as I sat across from Iris and looked at this beautiful woman, I wondered deep inside if either of us was ready for a relationship. It saddened me a little, as I was hoping things would be different with her and that maybe we could start something.

"What are you thinking about?" Iris questioned.

"Oh, just about you, your story and mine, and what the future may hold for us."

She smiled as she dug her fork into a large slice of blueberry cheesecake. "What does that look like for you?" she questioned. "The future?"

"Well, as much as I'd like to say I'd like to see you on an ongoing basis, I think perhaps we should just focus on a friendship for now."

Iris nodded. "I think I agree. I think that given your situation and mine, that perhaps friends would be best."

"I'm glad that you didn't take offence to that. I'm really trying to focus on a new normal for Grace and to do the right things. It's hard when there is another little human that you have to consider."

"Don't I know it? I told the boys I was going out with a friend tonight. I was afraid to tell them. I think we just need to focus on one day at a time, and if something progresses between us, then we deal with it then."

"I think that sounds perfectly reasonable."

Iris and I walked hand-in-hand to her car. Once there, she thanked me for a wonderful evening, and we set up our next coffee date and went on our separate ways home.

Since dinner and our mutual agreement to just remain friends, Zach and I had gotten to know one another very well. In those short two weeks we'd had dinner twice, coffee many times, and one evening I'd gone over to his place while the boys were at swim practice to help him choose the paint colour for one room in the inn. Our choice to stay just friends had taken away all the pressures we were putting on ourselves to impress one another.

This morning, I was meeting Zach for our coffee, so after I dropped the boys off at school, I headed into The Crispy Biscuit to find him already sitting in our usual booth. I walked over and sat down to see he had already ordered our coffees and our snacks.

"Sorry I'm late. It was an adventure getting those two

off to school this morning. Dylan had a massive attitude," I said, shrugging out of my sweater.

"Must be something in the air. Grace was full of attitude as well."

Zach looked exhausted. "How is everything else? You look wiped out."

"I am. This renovation is taking on a life of its own. My mother has been driving me crazy with more tile and flooring choices and dreaded paint choices. I will not lie, I'm glad to have the place to myself this weekend. Give me some time to think."

"Oh you too? The boys are going off to my sister's. It will be wonderful to have the quiet. Plus, I might actually get some time to myself to relax. Read a book or take a hot shower without being barged in on."

"Best part is, I have no contractors this weekend either, so the house will be quiet as well. What are your plans for relaxation?"

"Well, I was thinking of heading up to that spa. I keep seeing commercials for it, The Oasis Retreat. They have hot and cold plunge pools and a sauna and peace," I said, getting excited just thinking about it. "The hotel portion is apparently fabulous, walking trails and nature, and the best part, it's adults only."

Zach closed his eyes and leaned back against the back of the booth. "Sounds like heaven. I used to love connecting with nature. Haven't done it in a while, but I sort of remember what it felt like to be grounded."

I took a minute and thought about inviting Zach. Was it appropriate being we were doing the friend thing?

"I'm not sure if this is crossing a line, but I have a weekend pass for two people that Trinity got when her and Thomas went to this place a couple weeks ago. She gave it to me, thinking I'd be able to use it, so if you'd like, I can call and see if they will give us two rooms. The coupon I have is for one room, double occupancy, but Trinity said they weren't all that busy, and being they just opened, they were more than willing to offer other options to her and Thomas when they told them they weren't interested in options that they'd been given with the pass."

Zach sat back and picked up his coffee, taking a sip. I could see he was thinking about it, or perhaps he was trying to decide how to answer me. Maybe it wasn't his type of thing, or maybe he only wanted to keep our friendship for coffee dates and dinner. I watched his shoulders rise and fall, and then he placed his coffee down and a relieved look came over his face.

"You're sure I wouldn't be cramping on your personal time?" Zach asked.

I smiled. I didn't want to let on that I wasn't keen on spending the entire weekend alone. I also didn't want to let on that I'd invited Trinity, but she couldn't go this weekend as she had plans with Thomas and, well, my sister had already committed to taking the boys.

"You wouldn't be cramping on my personal time. I wouldn't have suggested it. It will be a nice getaway for the both of us, and from the looks of you, I think you may need this more than I do." I giggled.

Zach laughed and winked. "You might be right. Well, see what you can do, and if things seem good, then I'm up for it."

I'd tucked Noah into bed and shut off his light and now went into Dylan's room. It looked like a bomb had gone off in it, clothes everywhere, along with toys. I started picking up the clothes and throwing them into his hamper when he came into his room.

"What are you doing?" he questioned, going over to his bed.

"Cleaning up. I want to get this laundry done tonight so that you can pack in the morning."

He climbed into bed and watched me for a few minutes.

"What is it, Dylan?" I questioned.

"I don't want to go to Aunt Beth's this weekend," he said, crossing his arms.

I shook my head; I wasn't in the mood to deal with his defiance. He'd been trouble since he'd gotten home with the letter from the principal who was requesting a meeting with me on Monday. Apparently, Dylan was acting out in class, and the teacher had grown tired of it.

"Dylan, look. You are going to see your aunt and uncle. There is no debate about that. Now, why don't you tell me what is going on at school?" I said, sitting down on the edge of his bed, thinking of that letter.

"There is nothing to tell."

I frowned. I knew something was going on. I'd gotten a report last week from his teacher that his grades were slipping, and she'd mentioned the attitude as well. He'd also stopped wanting to go to the park to play with the other kids and had made Noah stay home as well.

"Dylan, your teacher and your principal seem to say different."

He leaned back against his pillow, and suddenly a tear formed in the corner of his eye, which he quickly wiped away before it escaped. I said nothing. Instead, I just watched him because I knew he was about to spill it, and sure enough, he let out a sigh and met my eyes.

"There's a boy who is picking on me."

"I see. What is he doing?"

"He found out we don't have a dad. He's been saying some really mean things."

Kids had always been cruel, and it appeared they were no different today than they were when I was in school. Dylan now was in full-blown tears as he lay in his bed, and my heart went out to him.

"Shhhh, it's okay. It will be alright, okay? I will have a word with the principal and your teacher," I said, pulling him for a hug.

"He'll just pick on me more," Dylan cried.

Now I wished I hadn't taken the boys out of school tomorrow to go with Beth. Instead, I wished I'd taken that appointment with the principal, but since our rooms were booked at the spa, I hadn't been able to.

"No, he won't."

"He will."

"Is he in your class?"

Dylan nodded.

"Is it one of the boys you used to play with after school down at the park?"

Dylan nodded again.

I wasn't going to pry it out of him. Whatever was going on, I'd find out all about it after the weekend.

"Okay, no more tears. You are going to go away with your aunt, uncle, and cousins this weekend and come Monday we will deal with all that. Sound good?"

Dylan nodded and wrapped his arms around me.

"Have a good time!" I said, kissing both my boys as my sister stood at the door waiting for them to grab their bags.

"We will." Dylan took his bag along with his brother's and headed out the door to where his uncle was standing waiting for them. Beth watched for a moment and then turned back to me.

"So, what are you going to do with yourself this weekend?"

"I'm going up to The Oasis Retreat," I said, my body already craving the quiet and relaxation the place promised.

"Ohhh Grant and I were just there for the day. It's wonderful. Are you—never mind," she said, stopping herself from asking whatever it was she was going to ask.

"Am I what?"

"Nothing, never mind," she said again.

"No, tell me."

Beth let out a sigh. "I was going to ask if you were going to be alone, but then I remembered that you and Zach decided to just be friends." The look of disappointment on her face said it all. I knew she wanted me to get involved with someone again, and I'd disappointed her with the news that we were just going to remain friends.

I couldn't help but smile. "Well, I won't be alone. He is going to come."

A look of excitement came over her face, and she was about to wrap her arms around me, but I stopped her.

"I invited him, only because he is dealing with a lot of things as well, and he looked like he could use a break. Don't get too excited. We have separate rooms," I said, fully stopping any ideas she may have of us falling into some sort of romantic venture for the weekend.

She gave me a look I'd never seen before and shook her head. "Maybe the gods of romance are in play after all," she said, rubbing her hands together.

"Just say nothing to the boys," I said.

"Never. I hope you have a good weekend. Call me if there are any issues."

"I will, have fun."

Zach

I'd gotten Grace off with my mother, and then I swung over and picked up Iris. We'd driven out to The Oasis Retreat. Iris went over to the front desk to check us in and get our keys, while I went to the washroom. When I returned, I noticed she was still at the desk, now looking frazzled.

She glanced over her shoulder and looked right at me, then turned back to the girl behind the desk and said something. I walked over, placing my hand on the small of her back to let her know I was there. She looked up at me, worry in her eyes.

"What is it?" I questioned. "Did they lose our reservation?"

"Something like that," she answered, watching the girl she'd been talking to speak with another employee. "They seem to have lost one of our rooms. They also informed me they are fully booked and apparently have no record of us needing two rooms."

I was about to try to calm Iris down when the girl approached the desk and placed the keys down on the counter. "So, we are indeed fully booked both today and tomorrow. We only have the room that was booked under your reservation number—a jacuzzi room, with one king bed. We unfortunately have nothing else."

I could sense Iris was on the verge of a breakdown but wasn't sure I should interfere.

"I don't understand. When I spoke to the agent I booked with yesterday, they assured me we'd have two rooms."

"I'm sorry, but without that email you said you received confirming the two rooms, we can't do anything. Not that we could anyway, because we have no other rooms available."

Iris looked up at me. I could tell she didn't want to be the one to answer or decide what to do, so I simply smiled and placed my hand over the keys on the counter.

"It's fine. The room will be fine," I said, giving her a gentle squeeze.

The girl behind the desk gave me a crooked smile as I grabbed our bags.

As we headed up the elevator to the fifth floor, Iris was quiet. I didn't want her to be upset. This weekend was one about relaxing, and that was what I'd planned to do. We made our way down the hall to the room, and I inserted the key and opened the door. We both stepped inside and looked around the large room.

"See, it's not so bad," I said.

"No, it's beautiful. It's just I swear to you I ordered two rooms."

I chuckled. "I believe you. This sort of stuff happens all the time," I said, trying to make her feel more at ease.

"It does?" she questioned.

"Sure." I laughed, not knowing what the hell I was talking about.

"To who?" she questioned.

"Well, it's never happened to me before, but I am sure someone out there has had something like this happen to them."

Iris looked at me and rolled her eyes and then laughed, and soon we stood there looking at one another in full-on laughter. "I guess it isn't the end of the world."

"Not at all. That bed is big enough for you, me, your boys, and Grace. We will be fine." I winked.

"So you aren't mad?

"Mad? God no, this isn't something to get mad about. I'm actually craving that hot tub I saw down there, so I'm heading down in a few minutes. What about you?"

Iris looked up at me, still a hint of worry in her eyes,

and smiled. "I'll be down. I'm just going to take a few minutes and make sure the boys are okay."

"Sounds good."

I lay in the hot water, my head back against the seat, and allowed myself to relax. The soft music that played just added to it. When I opened my eyes, I saw Iris walk in, wrapped in one of the white robes that were in our room. She glanced around and then spotted me. She made her way over to the side of the pool I was in and smiled.

"Okay if I join you?" she asked quietly so not to disturb the other guests in the area.

"Of course."

She looked around the room cautiously before slipping the robe off her shoulders to expose herself in a purple bikini. I tried not to allow my eyes to wander, but it was damn near impossible. Iris was an attractive woman with a body to match the personality and looks.

Within seconds she slipped into the water, her body hidden from view, which, at the moment, I was glad for. My eyes were glued to her as she leaned back against the seat and closed her eyes. I was harder than a rock just from looking at her, and when she let out a soft moan as she relaxed, it was almost my undoing.

"Relaxing isn't it," I said, swallowing hard while trying hard to focus on anything other than the sound of that moan, the look on her face, and my throbbing cock.

"Ohhh, god yes."

I felt like I'd been transported back to my teen years. This was ridiculous. Who'd have thought I'd be sitting here with my cock as hard as a rock in a hot tub with a half-naked woman who I was friends with? I'd resigned myself to the fact that there would be nothing between us, yet at this moment, I wanted to do nothing but kiss her pouty lips and make her moan exactly like that.

"That's good," I said, my voice cracking suddenly.

Iris still sat there with her eyes closed. She hadn't noticed my voice. I looked up at the roof and counted to ten; I had to distract myself from the thoughts that were floating through my mind.

"I'm going to hit that cold plunge over there," I said, as the people who'd been sitting in it just left to return to the other hot tub.

"Okay, I'll be here," she said, not opening her eyes.

Two hours later, I lay in the relaxation room overlooking the woods. This was supposed to be relaxing, but my mind hadn't shut off. All I kept thinking about was the reasons I had suggested why Iris and I shouldn't be together, yet none of them seemed to be good enough.

"There you are," I heard Iris say behind me.

"Yes, how was your massage?" I questioned, looking up at her.

"I haven't been this relaxed in ages," she said, letting out a yawn.

I chuckled. I'd begun feeling that way when I first sat in that heated hot tub, and then that faded as Iris sunk in beside me. I'd been on edge since, my body keyed up and ready for things it hadn't felt in ages.

"What time is dinner?" I questioned.

"Six."

"Alright, I'm going to go up and take a shower. Why don't you stay here for a bit and continue to unwind?" I suggested, nodding to the lounger beside mine. "Have a cucumber water. It's delicious."

She looked around the room and then at me and nodded. "I think I will."

Iris

I took my time walking through the lower part of the spa, stopping into a couple of stores on my way back to my room. Zach should be finished with his shower, and I'd have the room to myself to get ready for dinner tonight.

I'd watched him for a bit this afternoon, swimming laps in the pool after he'd left the cold plunge. I'd watched how the muscles in his back had contracted as he swam back and forth, and then how his abs flexed as he climbed the ladder out of the pool.

I'd been a fool to think that I'd be able to do this weekend. The man was a god, and there was no denying that I was attracted to him.

I slid the key card into the door lock and stepped inside. The room was quiet. I went over to my suitcase and pulled out the dress I'd brought for dinner, and then grabbed my toiletry bag from my suitcase and made my way into the washroom.

The room was still warm from when Zach had his shower. I moved the pile of towels from the front of the tub and placed a dry one on the floor. I slipped out of my stuff, leaving everything in a pile on the counter, and pulled back the curtain on the tub. In a flash my eyes landed on Zach, who stood naked before me, his large hard cock in his hand the other resting on the wall in front of him, a look of shock and embarrassment on his face as his eyes ran the length of my bare body.

"Oh my god!" I screamed, grabbing for a towel that

hung on the towel rack and quickly covering myself. It was too late, though. I knew he'd seen me, just like I saw him, as he quickly grabbed for the shower curtain that I'd ripped away from covering him.

We both stood there, looking at one another, our faces red, each one of us mortified in the moment. It was then I turned around, ripping my eyes from him.

"I thought you were downstairs. God, Zach, I'm so embarrassed. I'm so..." I took off from the bathroom, feeling like I could die. Panicking, I raced around the room, grabbing clothes from my suitcase as my heart raced until I felt faint.

I dropped my clothes to the floor and sat down on the bed, breathing hard, trying to erase what I'd just seen. I heard the bathroom door open and then felt the end of the bed dip down and a warm hand on my bare shoulder.

"Zach, please, this is just all too much," I said, my vision blurring as I looked out the window.

"Hey. It's alright. Look, I'm going to take a step back here, and I'd like you to do the same. Look at me."

I could barely turn my head, but I did, and when I met his eyes, I didn't see someone who was embarrassed. Instead, he looked at me with the same look he'd given me ever since we met.

"We are two adults. We are sharing a room. I know you didn't think I was in there. Hell, I didn't think you were back up here or were coming up anytime soon. So how about we both just forget what happened and try to have a good evening."

I swallowed hard. I still felt like I wanted to die, and here he was trying hard to ignore the fact that we'd seen one another in our birthday suits.

"Zach, I can't."

"You can. I know you can. Now I'm going to get dressed and leave you so you can get ready for dinner. I'll meet you in the lobby."

He didn't say another word. Instead, he did as he said he was going to.

Once he was gone, I reached for my cell phone. I needed help, and the only one I could think of was my sister. I dialed her number and waited for her to answer. Finally, on the fifth ring, she picked up, laughter in her voice.

"Hello!"

"Beth...it's Iris," I said, fighting back the tears that were threatening to fall.

"Iris?" The line went quiet for a moment. "Is everything alright?"

I didn't know how to answer that. I felt like I was going to fall apart. I'd seen another man naked, one other than my dead husband, and I felt as if the world—my world—was falling apart.

"Iris?" she repeated, her voice growing serious.

"Please tell me you are away from the boys?"

"Oh yes, they are outside in the backyard. What's wrong?"

I took in deep breath and blew out through my mouth, trying hard not to panic. "We um, I um...I walked in on Zach, and he was ummm..."

"Walked in on him, what? Iris, what is going on?"

"I walked in on him in the shower.... Masturbating," I loudly whispered.

I heard nothing on the end of the phone except for a door slamming shut. "Oh my god, spill it," Beth quietly shouted into the phone. "I thought you had separate rooms."

"So did I. However, when we got here, there was a screwup with our reservation. Anyway, he came up here to get ready for dinner and um, well, I thought he was already gone when I returned to the room, so I got ready to have a shower, and well, when I pulled the curtain back on the shower, there he was..."

Beth let out a loud laugh.

"I'm glad you are enjoying my pain, but god, I want to die."

"Oh, my god. Come on. Don't panic. It's just a penis."

If Beth had seen it, she'd have known it wasn't just a penis, but an amazing penis at that. Once again, the vision of him standing there stroking himself flashed before my eyes. His large hand wrapped tightly around himself, the muscles in his forearm flexing, his abs flexing as well, that deeply carved vee...

"Seriously, Iris, it was only a penis."

"Stop saying that," I said, swallowing hard as my sister continued to laugh. "It's also, I too was naked. I'd stripped out of my clothes before opening the shower curtain and..."

Beth continued to laugh. I didn't know whether I should hang up on my ever-so-supportive sister or continue telling her.

"Okay, big deal, so he may have seen you naked. Now what is it? Did you like what—"

"Don't you dare even ask me that. He's...we are supposed to be friends."

"Uh-huh. Friends, that is right. If you were only friends, you wouldn't be flipping out right now. Admit it, you like this guy."

I looked outside through blurry eyes. "No, absolutely not. We are only friends," I whispered.

"Iris, do yourself a favor. Do me a favor. Have a good time this weekend."

Just then, I heard voices coming through the phone and instantly recognized Dylan and Noah talking in the background.

"Don't let on it's me," I said. "I can't talk to them this way. They will know something is wrong."

"I'm not letting them talk to you. Go have fun. The

next time you call, I want to hear all about your adventures tonight. Do you understand what I'm telling you? Let loose, enjoy yourself. Hell, enjoy him. Live a little, or a lot."

I could imagine Beth standing there, a smile on her face.

"I'll talk to you later," I said.

"Have fun, sis. Seriously, enjoy that penis. I mean. Enjoy your time with your friend. Love you lots."

I held my cell phone for a moment and then laughed at what Beth had said. She was right. Perhaps I needed to live a little. If Zach wasn't embarrassed about it, why should I be? Only problem was, I was embarrassed by it.

I sat in the lounge, a drink in front of me, waiting for Iris to appear. Part of me feared she wouldn't after the mishap in the room a little over an hour ago. I was worried that the mishap would be the end of our weekend. So, it surprised me when I saw her finally step out of the elevator.

I was about to lift my hand when she spotted me and began heading in my direction. I thought it was adorable that her cheeks flushed as she approached me. Was she still embarrassed about the events that had transpired? I'd hoped not. In typical guy fashion, I'd liked what I'd seen. I certainly wasn't going to deny that.

She approached the table with caution, and I stood up, pushing the chair out and away from the table for her to sit down.

"I ordered you a gin and tonic. I hope that's okay?" I said, wanting to show her that nothing had changed on my side of things.

"Great, thank you," she said, her hands shaking as she placed her clutch bag on the table. "I could use it."

"I had them push our reservation back. Dinner is now at seven. I figured you might need a little more time after...."

Her eyes flew to mine. "Please, Zach, I'm so sorry about what happened. I feel so stupid for not knocking on the door before I went in and just assuming you had left the room."

I chuckled. "It's fine. Honestly. However, there is one thing I can't seem to get out of my mind."

I watched as her eyes fell to the floor.

"Oh, dare I ask." She muttered to herself. "What is that?" she questioned, resting her head on her hand.

"How sexy you looked."

Her cheeks flooded with colour, and she buried her face in her hands at my words.

"Oh god."

I leaned over and placed my hand on her thigh. "It's okay. Really, nothing to be embarrassed about. I'm the one who should be embarrassed." I chuckled.

Iris looked over at me, an embarrassed look on her face. The server approached our table and placed one drink in front of me and was about to set Iris's down when she grabbed hers and drank half of it right away. Then glanced at the server and asked for another.

The server glanced at me and then made her way back to the bar. The table grew quiet as I watched Iris devour the rest of that first drink and then placed the glass down on the table just as the server brought over the other one.

Iris leaned over toward me, her cheeks now fully fired up with color. "You have nothing to be embarrassed about," she whispered before picking up the next drink and proceeding to drink down the rest of that one as well.

The elevator doors opened, and I glanced up to see that we were on our floor. Iris was laughing hard at something I'd said on our way up here, and I grabbed her hand and gently guided her from the elevator before the doors closed.

"Shhhh. It's late," I whispered.

We'd closed the restaurant and had returned to the lounge where the music had been playing. We'd drank, talked, and even danced twice. However, a few minutes ago, they announced they were closing for the night, so we retired to our room. We walked down the hall and stopped outside our door while I dug into my pocket for the key. Iris rested her head on my arm while I worked with the finicky lock. We stepped into the dimly lit room to see a bottle of wine in a chiller on the table.

"What's this?" Iris asked nodding toward the table.

I frowned. "No idea." I made my way over toward her to see if there was any type of note left, but there was nothing.

"Huh, did you do this?" Iris questioned, looking up at me as I pulled the bottle out of the chiller and removed the cork and poured us each a glass.

"Nope, but we might as well enjoy it," I replied, placing the bottle back in the chiller. I picked up my glass and handed her the other.

"To us, a beautiful friendship, even if we have seen one another naked." I winked.

Iris let out a laugh as our glasses clinked together and took a drink. I was glad to see she was finally laughing at what had happened earlier.

"I think I'm going to get out of this dress. Give me a minute." She placed her glass back down on the table and headed to the washroom.

"Sure thing. Take your time."

I walked over and looked out the window. It seemed to take her longer than what would be normal, and I was about to knock on the bathroom door to see that she was okay when it opened, and Iris stuck her head out.

"Zach."

"Yeah?"

"Um, I hate to ask but my zipper is stuck. Would it be too much trouble for you to give me a hand?"

I walked over to the bathroom door and smiled as she poked her head out. "Not at all," I said, my voice low. "You may need to come out of there though, I'm not too good working through the door." I smiled.

She smiled and stepped out of the bathroom and turned around, where I could see the zipper had stopped a little less than the halfway point. I gripped the small zipper and pinched the fabric at the top and tried to pull, but the zipper wouldn't budge. I pulled it back up and tried again, and again it stopped in the same place.

"Can't get it?" she asked.

One more tug and it finally released. I looked up and caught her eyes in the mirror as I slowly unzipped the dress, my fingers skimming along the soft, bare skin of her back, her skin pebbling at my touch.

She was silent as she turned around in my arms and met my eyes. I didn't register what I even did next. I brought my hand to the straps of the dress and ever so gently slid them down her arms, letting the dress fall and pool at her feet. My eyes washed over her body as she looked up at me. I could see her hardened nipples through the material of her bra, and my cock hardened when I caught sight of the thong she wore in the mirror. She had a perfect round ass, one I could see myself gripping as she rode me.

She looked up at me, her cheeks flushed, and I felt her fingers playing with the buttons on my shirt. Slowly she undid them from the bottom up, and once they were all undone, she slipped her hands into my shirt and shoved it off my shoulders. I could see the want in her eyes, the burning, the aching to be taken.

I wrapped my arms around her, lifting her. She wrapped her legs around my waist, her arms around my neck, and crashed into my mouth. There was no denying it, I fucking wanted her, and I had to have her. I carried her over to the bed, placing her down in the centre, and held myself above her as I took her mouth again, this time parting her lips and running my tongue through her mouth. She tasted like heaven.

With one hand supporting me, I reached down and pulled at the button on my pants. I needed some sort of relief. These pants were too restrictive. I looked down at her and was surprised when she grabbed my hand, placing it on her breast.

I kissed her hard as I ran my fingers over her hardened nipple, then I pulled away, bringing my mouth down and sucking that perfect pink bud into my mouth. Her fingers slid through my hair as I did it again, this time gently biting, then flicking my tongue across it before moving to the other one. I kissed my way down her stomach, then moved to her inner thigh., while gripping her ass I kissed the inside of her legs.

"That feels so good," she muttered breathlessly.

"You like that?"

"Uh-huh."

My fingers lightly danced over the crotch of her panties. She was soaked. I pressed light enough to tease her, but not enough to provide any type of relief. Her sharp inhale told me to do it again, this time adding a little more pressure. I wanted to feel how soaked she was, so while kissing her thigh, I slid my fingers into her panties and ran my fingers through her centre.

"Ahhhh...god...." she moaned while squirming on the bed. "Do it again."

I gripped her panties, and she rose up a little so I could slide them off her. She lay completely naked before me, her eyes begging me for more.

I shoved at my pants and boxers, grateful when I sprung free, and gripped my aching cock as I moved between her legs. Again, I kissed the insides of her thighs as her fingers ran through my hair. I wanted to make her come undone. I gripped her hips and ran my tongue through her centre, relishing the sweet taste of her. Her fingers gripped my hair, and the loud moan told me to continue lapping and sucking.

"God, Zach."

A couple more flicks of my tongue against her clit and

I felt her body stiffen a bit. Her cries got louder, and finally she came undone in my arms. I moved up toward her and placed a kiss on her mouth while she lay there breathing hard. When she finally came down, she looked at me and down to my hand which was slowly stroking my cock. The second her hand touched me, I closed my eyes and let her take over.

I bit my lower lip and closed my eyes as she finally wrapped her hand around me. It felt like fucking heaven as she stroked my entire length. She ran her thumb over the drop of precum that sat on the head of my cock, rubbing into the soft skin. Then I felt her sink her hot mouth onto me and I almost lost it.

Concentrating on her mouth, her hand as she stroked me, I felt my orgasm building at the base of my spine. It was only a matter of minutes before I found my hand wrapped in her hair as she swallowed down every drop of me.

The room was blurry as I opened my eyes, blinking twice, trying to clear the sleep from my eyes. I was warm and comfortable. It felt like my body had melted into the mattress as I closed my eyes and let out a yawn. I felt Zach slip his hand into mine, and the memory of last night came rushing back.

"Morning," he said, pressing a kiss to the side of my neck.

"Morning."

I closed my eyes and relished being held by this man. We'd spent the night wrapped in one another's arms, both of us now fully satiated. He was quiet. I could feel the light puff of his breath on my neck as he fell back to sleep. I locked my fingers with his and lay there thinking about what would happen after we left here today.

Last night had happened. I'd taken my sister's advice after a few too many drinks and had let go and had fun. Did I regret it? No. However, we'd both agreed to remain friends and only friends, and I felt that this would throw some sort of wrench in the gears.

I closed my eyes, my memory instantly flashing back to earlier this morning as I gripped the headboard as he pounded into me from behind, his hand wrapped in my hair just tight enough to pull my head back.

"What are you thinking about?"

I'd been so lost in that moment, I could feel myself getting aroused again, my body betraying me as I thought about it, that I jumped at the sound of his voice.

"Nothing, why?"

His fingers danced over my bare skin, then he gripped my hip and pulled me tighter into him, his cock already hard.

"If you are thinking about what I was thinking about, then this might end up disastrous," he whispered, his breath tickling my neck.

He moved enough that he rolled onto my body, and his lips immediately met mine. I closed my eyes as he kissed me, and his hands explored my body for what I was certain would be the last time. Soon, we'd both be back in our realities, and I wasn't sure if this weekend would only become a glorious memory or something that would continue.

"Alright, Noah, here, this is your box," I said, pulling the large box from the closet and handing it to him.

"Where is mine?" Dylan questioned, coming out of his room with an empty one.

"Hmmm, this one, right here," I said, reaching into the closet and grabbing one with my name on it.

"Oh yes! Finally!" Noah yelled from his room in excitement.

I giggled, knowing full well that the contents of that box contained all the toys he'd been asking me for, for weeks. "That is the box you wanted, right, Noah?" I yelled, peeking into his room to see him dancing around as he put things away.

"I never thought I'd see them again!" he yelled back to me as I carried another one of my boxes into my room and placed it on the bed.

It had been weeks and weeks of unpacking boxes. Some things were still in the storage unit, as it was hard to fit all these boxes into a house twice as small. I'd made a deal with the boys to get rid of the things we were no longer using to help clear out the unit faster. So far, they had come up with three boxes of toys each, and I'd gotten rid of five boxes. I'd made them a deal that we would run a yard sale in the fall and that they could keep all the money from the things they'd sold. I wanted to motivate them. So far, it had worked.

I wandered back into my bedroom and continued unpacking. Zach and I returned this morning and said our goodbyes. We'd talked the entire way home about what had happened over the weekend. We both agreed that while it had been wonderful, now wasn't the time for it to continue. I'd be lying if I said I wasn't disappointed.

I glanced at my cell phone, hoping to have a message from him, but there was nothing. I let out a sigh and went back to the box that was in front of me. I was about to unwrap the next item when I heard the boys whispering in the hallway just outside my door. I listened hard, trying to hear what it was they were saying, but couldn't quite make it out. Then, suddenly, Dylan stumbled into the doorway.

I glanced over at him with a frown on my face. "What's up?" I questioned.

He folded his hands together and stood there with his head bowed.

"Ask her," Noah demanded, shoving him in the shoulder. "We need to know."

"What is it, Dylan?"

The boys were still acting out. Beth told me last night they'd gotten into a fight at the dinner table. Today they'd gotten into a fight with two neighbourhood boys. This was so unlike these two, I was worried. I'd asked them both what the fight had been about, but neither would tell me. I'd thought about asking Zach to come and have a talk with them, figuring they may tell him because he's a man, but decided against it. They just each went to their rooms and slammed the doors shut.

I waited for Dylan to speak, but he didn't. He just stood there with his eyes on the floor until his brother shoved him in the shoulder again.

"Don't shove me."

Immediately, I walked out to the hall and stood between them. "What is going on?" I demanded.

"Dylan wants to know if it's true?" Noah piped up.

"If what is true?"

"What the boys are saying at school? That our mother is dating the man who now lives at the bed and breakfast."

I blew out a breath. This was one thing I hated about small towns. Gossip.

"Where did you hear that?"

"Some boys at school were talking."

"I see. Is it the same boy you told me about, the one bullying you?" I demanded, thinking back to the other night before the boys left to visit their aunt. Only neither of them said a word.

"We want to know why you lied to us," Dylan demanded. "You always told us not to lie to you."

I blew out a breath. I hadn't lied. I just hadn't told the

whole truth, but I also couldn't tell them that because I'd just gotten angry at both the boys for that very thing. Letting out a sigh, I ushered both boys into my bedroom and had them sit down.

"Listen, I went out with Zach for dinner. Yes. I told you I was going out with a friend because I was afraid you both weren't ready to hear about me going out with another man."

"Meh, don't bother me any," Noah said, hopping off the bed. "Have fun, Mom." He took off toward his room.

That had gone way better than I expected. However, he was only seven. I couldn't imagine that he'd understand fully. However, when I turned back around, Dylan sat there, his head down.

"What's up, sweetie?" I questioned.

He shrugged but said nothing.

I watched as he reached over and grabbed the wedding photo that I I kept on my bedside table. He picked it up and looked at it, running his little fingers over Lucas's face.

I slowed my unpacking and watched him, concern filling me. "Dylan, you know you can talk to me if something is bothering you."

He let out a sigh and looked up at me with tears in his eyes. "I don't understand. Do you not love Dad anymore?"

My stomach sank at his words. It didn't hit me until just then that for the first time in my life I'd slept with another man, not that the boys needed to know this. I swallowed hard, trying to wipe the memory of this past weekend from my mind as I watched Dylan sitting there holding our photo.

"Dylan..."

"You don't do you? Now that he is gone, you're just trying to replace him."

"Dylan, you know that isn't true."

"I don't, Mom."

"Dylan, I am not looking to replace him. I spent many years with your father, and I loved him very much, and still love him deeply. I don't expect you to understand how hard this has been on me. I also don't expect you to understand that eventually I have to move on with my life."

"You're right, I don't understand."

"I hope you never have to understand this. I can promise you I am not trying to replace him. Zach and I... well, we are just friends."

As the words fell from my lips, I realized I wasn't sure that was what I wanted from him. I liked how he'd made me feel in more ways than one. I'd loved everything about the other night, how I felt in his arms, how he made me feel while rocking my world.

Dylan shook his head. "That isn't what Johnny said.

He said the same thing happened with his mom when his dad left, and soon he had a new dad, whether he wanted one or not. He said the same thing was going to happen to us."

I got up from the edge of the bed and went out into the hall and called Noah back into the room. Once they were both sitting on the edge of my bed, I stood in front of them, pacing back and forth for a couple of minutes, trying to figure out how to explain things to them in a way they'd understand.

"Listen, I promise you both I still love your father, and I will always love your father. I also promise you I am not and will not try to replace him. I went out with Zach for dinner as a friend. He needs someone, as he lost his wife as well. They divorced. We had a great time, and we aren't boyfriend and girlfriend. In fact, far from it," I said, swallowing hard and denying myself the fact that I'd love it if he were in my life as something more.

"We are simply two people who enjoy one another's company, and we are there for one another if the other needs to talk."

"So, you aren't trying to replace Dad?" Dylan questioned.

I shook my head. "Never could. He and I shared a lot of special moments together. He gave me a wonderful life. Plus, he gave me both of you," I said, kissing each one of them on the cheek, trying hard to reassure them that things were fine. "Now, I think it's time that we all unpack a couple more boxes and then we head on out for some ice-cream. What do you say?"

"I want chocolate!" Noah screamed. "Two scoops."

I laughed. "Alright, I left two boxes for each of you in the hallway with your name on it. Go get them, unpack them, and let's get going."

The boys each took off out to the hall and grabbed their boxes, while I turned back to the one I'd been working on. My stomach flipped when I looked down to see my phone lighting up Zach's name on the screen. My heart sank at the decision we'd made. Instead of looking at the message, I ignored it.

I sat down and looked out in the hall toward the boys' rooms. Zach and I were only friends. We'd decided on that this morning. We were both adults, and we'd both given the other a chance to voice how they felt. When neither one said anything, we decided that we'd pack this past weekend away in our memories, because it seemed more reasonable than trying to get into a relationship with someone when things were in utter chaos in both our lives. However, now, the more I thought about the weekend, the more I wanted to be more than friends. I had from the time he'd asked me out.

I got up and grabbed the next item from the box just

as my cell phone lit up again. This time when I saw his name, I stopped what I was doing and picked it up. I would not deny myself what I wanted. I'd just figure this out as I went.

Zach

"Hello," Iris's voice came over the phone.

It was like music to my ears, hearing the excitement in her voice when she heard mine. Since I'd dropped her off, I'd been wanting some time with her. I wanted to make sure she was okay after how we'd left things. Not that they were left in a bad way, but I felt uneasy after spending the night with her. It wasn't my style to have sex with someone I wasn't involved with.

"Hey, how are things going?" I asked.

"Not too bad. You're lucky, a few minutes earlier and you would have caught me in the middle of an inquisition."

"Inquisition? What happened?"

The line went quiet, and I sat there doodling on a

piece of paper while waiting for her to come back. I heard her clear her throat.

"Remember how I said that I got a note from the principal at school?"

"Yeah."

"Well, the boys finally told me what is going on. There are apparently some rumors flying around town. Some of the neighborhood boys have apparently heard that we were on a date the other night. I guess one boy they play with was at the Italian Affair with their parents and they told Noah and Dylan that they saw me there with you."

"Oh no. That sounds brutal. Grace asked me where I was going that night as well. She questioned why I was dressed so nice. It's fun being questioned by a minor, isn't it?" I laughed.

"Sure is. However, I fear my two were more worried about bigger things. Things that they didn't need to be."

"Dare I ask?" I chuckled, wondering what on earth they could be worried about.

Again, the line went quiet, and I sat waiting for her to answer me.

"Well, they were afraid that I was going to replace their father and that I didn't love him anymore."

I whistled into the phone. "So young with such big questions. Are you doing okay?"

While I waited for her to answer me, I couldn't help but wonder if perhaps she wasn't okay with our agreement on friendship. Only hours ago, we were locked away in a hotel room wrapped in one another's arms. A place I wanted to be again so badly. Now, thinking about what she'd just said, I worried that perhaps this weekend may have been a little much for her. I wasn't sure what to expect now.

"Yeah, I just wasn't expecting that," Iris answered. "Kind of upset me to think that they would even think I could even do that. However, I don't see the world through the eyes of a child, so I can sort of understand where they are coming from."

"True. Are the boys okay now?"

The phone went quiet again, but I could still hear Iris breathing on the other end. "I sure hope so. I explained to them that wasn't my plan, and I assured them I still loved their father. I just hope that they believed me. They have been out of sorts since we went out."

I shoved my hand into my pocket and paced the kitchen. I didn't want Iris to be dealing with these things alone. I totally sympathized with her situation. Those boys had lost a father figure in their life, at a young age. Iris was dealing with many things, not just her own feelings. She was trying to navigate raising those boys alone, just like I was raising Grace on my own. We both had been strong for them.

"Listen, I was thinking maybe we could meet for a coffee later?"

"I think I could do that." I could hear the smile on her lips.

"Alright, say tomorrow morning after the kids are in school? Our usual?"

"Sounds good. I'll see you then."

The next morning, I got Gracie off to school, but not without a fight. She fought me on every little thing. First it was breakfast, then it was getting dressed, then it was getting in the car. I'd never been so grateful to drop her off. I stepped into the diner and immediately saw Iris sitting in the back corner, a menu in front of her. She looked gorgeous in a burgundy sweater, her hair pulled back neatly in a bun. I nodded toward her table and then made my way over, Melinda following with a menu.

"I'll take a coffee," I said to Melinda, then turned to Iris. "Morning."

"Morning. How'd things go this morning? You look frazzled."

I chuckled. Frazzled wasn't the word. I was exhausted. "Oh, you know, just one big argument after another."

"Girls can be hard. Just wait until she hits her teens," Iris said, nodding in understanding. "Almost as hard as boys, only with far more attitude."

"That they can, and no offense, but girls are way harder."

She laughed. "None taken, and you are probably right."

"How were the boys?"

Iris grabbed the sugar and added a couple of teaspoons to her coffee. "Not bad, I'm sure, though it's not over. Like I said, they have been fighting a lot since the other boys have been picking on them. They have even been fighting amongst themselves, which was something they never did. I just hope it's temporary."

"I'm sure. You know, after we spoke last night, I was thinking. Why don't we make plans to get the kids together for a day? That way, Gracie can get to know you, and I can get to know Noah and Dylan. We can take them down to the water, they can fish, swim, and we can even take a picnic lunch. You know, make the day for them."

Iris sat there stirring her coffee. I could see hesitation on her face. I wanted to ask what it was she was thinking but didn't. Finally, she nodded. "I think that would be wonderful. It will give us time to spend the day together. I mean, not us as in you and me, besides I think the boys need it," she said, avoiding my eyes now.

The way she had changed direction of what she was saying made me worry she wasn't okay with what had happened between us, and I wanted to ask her but knew this wasn't the place.

"How is Sunday? I have dates with contractors all week. Lord knows I'll need the downtime."

Iris pulled her phone from her purse and opened her calendar, finally nodding. "Sunday works."

"Perfect. How about Gracie and I pick you up and we'll go from there."

"Alright. I'll pack the picnic lunch."

I lay in bed, going over some financial statements that the contractors had left for me, but I was having a hard time concentrating.

Ever since I'd returned from coffee this morning, the only thing on my mind had been Iris and the weekend we'd spent together. I feared I'd made it difficult for her, especially now that the boys were asking such tough questions. I rested my head against the headboard and thought about how her face had lit up when I'd suggested we get together this weekend. I tried to focus back on the statements, then put the pencil down and picked up my phone and quickly typed out a message to Iris. Then deleted it, throwing my phone back down.

When we'd left The Crispy Biscuit today, I'd wanted to kiss her. Fuck, I stood there, feeling the softness of her lips on mine, yet couldn't do a damn thing about it because we'd made some silly agreement to be friends. Who the hell was I. After the weekend we'd spent together, I must have been out of my mind to make an agreement like that.

I ran my hand over my face and picked up my phone, trying to figure out how to ask her if she still felt the same way as I did, but I didn't want to appear to be pushy.

Instead of texting, I dialed her number. It rang, and the second she answered, I got nervous and hung up. It was like I was some stupid teenager asking a girl out for the first time, not a man who'd walked down an aisle with one woman.

Seconds later, my phone vibrated, and I looked down to see a text message from Iris.

> Iris: Some weirdo called and hung up just as I answered. Any ideas?

Yep, it was me, and I'm a huge-ass chicken, I thought to myself.

> Zach: Huh

> Iris: number said it was you. Any ideas? ;)

> Zach: Must have been Gracie playing with my phone.

> Iris: At eleven pm, I'd really like to hope she's sleeping by now, or she'll be a monster in the morning. I know how much you love that!

> Zach: Okay, confession, the hangup was me. :|

> Iris: :P What's up? Is everything okay?

I tapped my phone. What was wrong with asking the woman a question? Was I afraid of the answer? Was I afraid she'd turn me down? Damn right I was. I closed my eyes, counted to ten, and then typed out what I wanted to know and hit send without thinking about it.

> Zach: Yeah, I was just wondering something, but I don't want you to think I'm pressuring you.

> Iris: Okay?

I rested my head back against the headboard and closed my eyes. I didn't want her to be angry at what I was going to ask. I wanted her to be open to the idea of an us.

> Zach: Promise me that if you don't want to talk about it, you'll just say so? I'll leave it at that in the future.

> Iris: Ummm....I sort of have to know what it is we are talking about before I promise you.

> Zach: Well, I just want to make sure you know you can be honest with me.

> Iris: Zach, care to tell me what this is all about.

> Zach: The night at the restaurant we decided to keep this as a friendship, then this past weekend happened and...

I watched those little dots bounce around for what felt like forever, and finally her response appeared.

> Iris: Yes, I remember.

> Zach: What if I want more than that?

I was holding my breath as those three little dots jumped around on my screen. They bounced, then they stopped and then they started again. My throat grew tight, and I wished I had said nothing because judging from the length of time I'd been waiting for a response, she obviously didn't feel the same way. Those three little torturous dots continued jumping.

> Zach: You can just ignore my question.

I put my phone down on the bed and ran my hands through my hair. I'd been stupid to even think that she'd wanted something. When I heard my phone ding, I didn't look at it right away, but when it went off a second, then a third time, I finally picked it back up.

Iris: Do you want more?

Iris: Am I reading this correctly?

Iris: Judging from the lack of response, I fear that I probably shouldn't admit that I, too, have been wondering how you might feel about us.

A smile came to my face as I read her reply.

Iris: ...maybe I was wrong for suggesting that we keep it platonic, especially after this past weekend. I'm embarrassed to say that I can't seem to forget about what happened between us.

Iris: Say something?

Zach: I hope we can have a repeat sometime soon.

Zach: I can't wait to see you on Sunday.

Iris: Same.

Zach: Talk to you soon.

Iris: Yes. Night Zach.

Zach: Night.

I placed the phone down beside me and picked up the financial statements, putting my focus on what I'd been working on earlier. My phone rang, and I grabbed it.

"So, you can't seem to stop thinking about the things we did on the weekend," I said into the phone, thinking that it was Iris. Only when I heard the voice on the other end, I froze.

It was Valerie.

"Fuck I missed you," Zach whispered just before his lips crashed against mine.

I lay beneath him, my fingers gripping his back as he pumped into me.

"I missed you too," I whispered back as he kissed my neck, pumping harder, our hands interlocked together as we both were pushed over the edge.

Half an hour later, I lay wrapped in his arms and closed my eyes while he ran his fingers up and down my bare arm.

"That feels nice," I said, placing a kiss on his chest.

Zach and I had seen one another every day this week, each time ending this way. I was just about asleep when his cell phone went off. He held me tight to him.

"Not again," he muttered as he picked up his phone and read the message that was waiting for him.

His phone had been going off for the last half an hour, both of us too wrapped up in one another to care.

"It's my mother. Contractor emergency," he said, kissing me. "Guess that means I have to go."

"I was hoping for round two," I said, pouting, pressing my lips against his.

"Come on. Not fair." He chuckled, slipping his arm out from under me and sitting up, reaching for his shirt and pants.

I did the same, then walked him to the door. I watched as he walked down the front walkway and climbed into his truck. He gave a wave and pulled out of the driveway, heading back to his place.

I walked into the kitchen and poured myself a cup of coffee. I had a few hours still until the boys got home and figured I'd just putter about cleaning. I'd just filled the bucket with hot water to wash the floor when my cell phone rang. I frowned when I saw it was the school.

"Hello."

"Iris, it's Devon Miller. I sent home a letter with Dylan a week ago. I need you to come in to the school today. It appears Dylan has been in a fight."

I closed my eyes. That call had erased every single blissful feeling I'd been holding onto.

"I'll be there as soon as I can."

It had been a long day, and I hadn't realized it until I sat down and took a sip of my coffee before I'd left to meet with the principal. Today was the last straw. The meeting with the principal hadn't gone well. Dylan had gotten into a fight and bloodied up a kid's nose at recess, and his teacher was at the end of her rope with his attitude. I had a good mind to call Zach and cancel for Sunday but didn't. Instead, I came home, threw in a load of laundry, and decided to see how the rest of today went.

I took my coffee into the living room and started working on unpacking one of the last boxes when the boys came through the door, dropped their bags, and headed to the kitchen for an after-school snack. I listened for signs of an argument, but they said nothing, and in they came each with a granola bar and a glass of soda.

"Unpacking still?" Dylan asked as he flopped down in the chair and turned the TV on.

"Yep. Nearing the end. It will be nice to be finished."

I reached into the box and pulled out a pile of photo albums and placed them on the table. Then I sifted through them, finally coming to the last one. I stared down at the cover. Bride and Groom were written in scrolled gold lettering, and my stomach did a flip. I'd packed it away so long ago I'd forgotten what box I'd put it in. As I pulled more from the box, I kept glancing at it. I didn't want to open it. I could barely even look at it, so I shoved it beneath the pile just as Noah wandered over and sat down.

"Is that my baby book?" he asked, pointing to one of the blue ones in the stack.

"Ummm...let me check," I said, opening the cover. "No, this one is Dylan's. This one is yours." I pulled the second one from the stack.

"Can I look at it?" he questioned, his eyes full of curiosity.

I looked at him and finally nodded. "Just be careful. There are some things in there I don't want to lose."

I placed the book on the table in front of him and watched as he carefully opened it, acting as if it were some sort of pop-up book.

"What about mine?" Dylan asked, coming over to the table.

"Sure, just like Noah. Be careful, okay?" I said, placing the book on the table in front of him.

While they flipped through their books, I focused on emptying the rest of the box, not thinking about the album I'd left sitting there. I placed another book down on top of the white album just as Dylan looked over.

"Can we look at this one?" he asked, pointing to the white one.

"Hmmm, I don't think so, sweetie," I said, grabbing it, planning to tuck it high into a cupboard.

"Come on, Mom. Please."

I turned around and looked at him. His eyes were so full of sadness and questions that I didn't have the heart to say no. "Okay," I answered, placing the book down on the table. "Make sure your hands are clean."

I took their glasses of soda and moved them to another table, then opened the book. Then I made my way back over to the box I'd been unpacking. I wasn't sure I could look at the album. It had been so long.

"Aren't you going to look at it with us, Mom?" Noah asked.

"Boys, I have lots to unpack," I said, my voice cracking.

"Just take a few minutes, please."

I closed my eyes and composed myself, then turned around, smiled, and walked over to stand between them as they flipped to the next page in the book. In a matter of seconds, I was transported back to the day of our wedding, and soon my eyes blurred with tears as I stared down at our photos.

"You looked so pretty. Did Dad think so?"

I smiled. "He did. He said the second he saw me, I took his breath away," I said, thinking back to that day. That was one of the things I could remember.

"You tried to strangle him?" Noah questioned.

I couldn't help but laugh at his smile. "No, it's just a saying."

The boys continued flipping pages, asking me questions. The more they asked, the harder it became. I'd never been so happy when they finally came to the last page of the album. I grabbed the books and neatly stacked them.

"Awww, Mom, can't we look at it again?" Noah questioned.

I shook my head. "Why don't you guys go do your homework while I get dinner ready?"

"Ahhh, Mom," Dylan moaned.

"Come on. Go on."

They both got up, grabbed their bags while I took the albums and shoved them into the back of one of cupboards in the living room. They stomped up the stairs, grumbling as they went.

Once I was alone, I turned back and looked at the cupboard I'd shoved those albums in. I quietly went over and opened it up, reaching in for our wedding album. I ran my hand over the cover and sat down, slowly opening it. With each turn of every page, I grew more and more upset, and soon I was sitting there with tears streaming down my face. I quickly wiped at the tears and continued flipping through the pages.

My chest was heavy and my heart hurt. After looking at these pictures, I realized there was no way I was ready to be involved with anyone yet. This album, the memories floating around, and the lack of them proved it.

I took the album and shoved it back into the cupboard. I grabbed a tissue, blew my nose, and wiped the tears from my cheeks. Now I needed to figure out how to break it to Zach.

I picked up my phone and quickly texted Zach, letting him know that we'd have to cancel our plans for Sunday. There was no reason attached. It was a simple we can't make it. Before I put my phone down, I turned the volume all the way down and placed my phone in my purse, hoping the old out of sigh out of mind would erase him from my mind for a while. Then I got up and went to the kitchen to prepare dinner.

We were all in the living room in our pajamas watching a show about sharks when Dylan rolled over and looked at me. "Mom, you said you had a surprise for us on Sunday. What is it?"

Instantly, my stomach sank. I'd forgotten I'd told them I had a surprise outing planned for Sunday. Now that I'd cancelled plans with Zach, I had nothing planned, but I had two boys who were looking forward to doing something.

"Yeah, Mom, you said we'd love the surprise," Noah said, sitting up on his knees, looking my way. "Can we know what it is now?"

"Yeah, about that..." I muttered, not sure how to go about telling them the plans had been canceled. I tried coming up with something to take them to on the fly, only my mind came up blank. The fall fair wasn't until the weekend after next, and anything fun, like mini putt or bowling, we'd have to go into Cedar Landing to do.

"Come on, Mom, tell us," Dylan said, sitting up and turning his full attention to me, even though the show he'd been wanting to watch was back on.

I was just about to explain to them I'd cancelled when a knock came at the door. I frowned and looked at each of them. It was odd that someone would knock at this time of night.

"Who is it, Mom?" Noah asked, looking over at the door.

"Yeah, who is it?" Dylan questioned.

I shrugged. "I don't have a clue. I'm not expecting anyone."

I got up out of my chair and made my way to the door. "Boys, just go back to watching your show."

"What if you need protection?" Dylan said, jumping up and flexing his arms.

I waved at Dylan, trying not to laugh. "I'll be fine. Watch your show."

Both boys turned their attention back to the TV. I glanced through the side glass panel to see Zach standing there. I frowned and pulled the door open.

"Hey," I whispered, not wanting to distract the boys.

"Can I come in?" he questioned.

I glanced over to see that both boys were still watching the show and not paying any attention to what was going on at the door. I nodded and opened the door, letting him step inside. We headed into the kitchen.

"Is everything okay?" I asked, grabbing my robe off the back of the kitchen chair, and throwing it over my flannel pajamas.

"Sorry to barge in like this. I tried messaging you after I got your text, but you didn't answer. I got a little worried," he said, taking my hands in his.

He held my hand for a couple of seconds before I pulled away from him. The fire that grew in my body from his touch made me feel guilty. Pretending like things were fine, I walked over to the kettle and switched it on. "Sorry, I shut my phone off. Did you want a coffee?"

"Sure." The room grew quiet. "Iris, is everything

okay?" he asked, this time coming over and placing his hands on my upper arms.

Again, I shrugged out of his touch, going to the fridge to grab the cream.

"Yeah, of course. I'm just tired is all. It's been a long week, and I just thought Sunday might be better spent unpacking. We only have a couple more days' worth of boxes as it is."

Zach frowned and sat down in the chair across from me. "Iris, are you sure everything's okay? This doesn't sound right. You were excited to go this morning."

I nodded and opened the cupboard, pulling down a couple of mugs. When I turned back around, I followed his gaze to the picnic basket I'd left on the counter. There was no way he was going to believe that I'd just changed my mind, because he was right. We'd talked about it almost every day this week. He'd known I'd gotten things for lunch. When he looked back over at me, his face fell.

"I'm sorry, but I'm having trouble understanding this. Have the boys been misbehaving?"

I shook my head. I hadn't mentioned to Zach about being called to the school this afternoon. "No, quite the opposite."

Zach glanced around the kitchen. The amount of confusion on his face was almost too much for me to take. This wasn't fair to him.

"Iris, give me a bone here. I'm confused. Gracie is excited and ready to go."

I turned away from him, trying to figure out a way to explain how I was feeling, when I heard Dylan's voice.

"Mom?"

I turned around to see both boys poking their heads around the corner and looking into the kitchen, both of them eyeing Zach with curiosity. I swallowed hard. I wasn't sure how they would react to seeing Zach here, especially after the way the boys at school had been teasing them.

"Boys, it's okay. You can come in. I'd like you to meet Zach," I said, figuring out that now was as good a time as any.

I watched as they cautiously made their way into the kitchen as Zach turned toward them. "Noah, Dylan. I'm Zach. Nice to meet you. I've heard a lot about you both."

Dylan gave half a wave, while Noah hid behind his brother, acting like he was a shield.

"Hey, Zach. Nice to meet you," Dylan finally said, coming to my side. "You are Grace's dad."

I met Zach's eyes.

"That I am."

Wrapping my arms around them both, I knelt, looking at them. "Boys, it's time for bed. Now, why don't you go up and brush your teeth and crawl into bed? You can each read for one hour, then I'll come in and tuck you both in."

"Okay." Both boys wrapped their arms around my neck and hugged me, then they waved to Zach and made their way upstairs.

I made our coffee and then sat down at the table with Zach and wrapped my hands around my mug.

"Are you going to tell me why you had the change of heart?"

"Promise you won't be angry."

"Why would I be angry?"

I looked around the kitchen, my leg bouncing up and down from nerves. "I um, I was unpacking some things earlier and came across my wedding album. It stirred up a lot of memories, and well, made me have second thoughts about all of this."

Zach nodded in understanding. "That would do it, I suppose. Why didn't you just tell me that? Tell me how you were feeling instead of flat out cancelling?"

I took a sip before answering. "It was easier than trying to explain. Plus, I thought you wouldn't understand, you know?"

"Try me. Give me a chance to understand."

"Okay, well..." I got up from the table and paced back and forth across the kitchen floor, ringing my hands together.

"Take your time. I'm listening."

I glanced over to the bottom of the stairs to make sure the boys weren't there. Then I turned to Zach.

"Something happened this week, inside of me, that I am having trouble with."

"Okay, like something physical?"

"No, more um, more mental and emotional."

Zach said nothing. Instead, he picked up his mug, took a drink, and waited for me to continue.

"Tonight, when I looked at that album, looked at those pictures, I panicked. I realized I couldn't remember what it felt like to be held by Lucas anymore. I was staring at a picture of us on our wedding day, his arms wrapped around me, and it was like I was looking at another couple. I couldn't hear his voice in my head or remember what he smelled like. I can barely remember how it felt like to be kissed by him. Then the boys, they were asking me questions, and I made up all the answers because I didn't have a clear enough view of that day to remember the things." I could feel the tears starting, and before I could fight them off, they were streaming down my cheeks.

I buried my face in my hands and sobbed. Moments later, I felt Zach wrap his arms around me, and I turned and buried my face in his chest.

"I'm not going to stand here and tell you I understand because I don't, but know that I've got you," he whispered, pulling me in tight, comforting me.

"That's the problem," I muttered.

"What is?"

"You've got me. While I was trying to remember all those things, all I could remember was you. Your touch, your kiss, your scent. Not only did it make me feel as if I lost him all over again, but I'm afraid of the feelings I have for you already. It's the first time I've felt alive since before Lucas died. It's almost like it's too much emotion."

"I get that. I feel it too, and if I am being honest, it scares me too. Needing to learn how to trust someone again isn't easy, just like it's difficult to allow yourself to become invested in someone else after such a tragic loss without being afraid that something bad will happen," Zach soothed.

I cried into his chest again as he held me. He understood exactly how I was feeling, which scared me even more than the rest of it. He was so understanding and patient, exactly what I'd hoped he'd be, because that was exactly what I'd needed. I wiped my cheeks and pulled away from his embrace.

"Wow, never did I think of telling you all that. I didn't think you'd be open to listening to this." I sniffled.

"Listening is who I am. Part of any relationship is good communication, and if we are ever going to have any type of relationship, friendship or otherwise, communication is where it is at. I never want you to feel you can't be honest with me. That was how the problems started in my marriage. I never realized that she wasn't happy. Hell, I didn't realize I wasn't happy until Grace was already born, and Valerie was sleeping with our neighbor.

"I try now to look at both sides and give an answer. It may not be the answer either of us wants to hear, but at least it's an answer and doesn't leave me or you wondering if we have done something."

I thought about what he'd said and nodded. I'd gone about it wrong, and now that I sat across from him, looking him in the eyes, I knew it. The hurt was there because I'd reacted purely to the emotions I was feeling at the moment.

"I'm sorry, Zach. I guess I got caught up in my emotions. It was wrong."

Zach reached out and took my hand in his. "Not wrong. This is new to both of us, and I can only imagine how hard it is to navigate how you are feeling. So, if you want to pass on Sunday, just say the word and we will take it from here."

I shook my head. "No, I want to go." I gripped his hand tighter and smiled, thankful that he was so understanding. We sat together and talked a little while longer about Sunday, and once his cup was empty, he got up and grabbed his coat.

"Wait." I held up my finger and got up out of my seat and went to the bottom of the stairs. "Before you go..."

I could still see the boys had their lights on, so I called

for them to come down. They both appeared a few moments later and wandered slowly into the kitchen.

"Boys, remember you asked me earlier about the surprise on Sunday?" I questioned.

Both boys looked from me to Zach and slowly nodded their heads.

"Well, Zach and I thought it would be fun if we all went on a picnic down by the water. We can fish and swim and you can get to know Gracie, Zach's daughter, a little more. What do you say?"

"Really, we can fish?" Noah asked.

I nodded and smiled at them, praying they didn't flip out over the fact that Zach would be going.

"But you can't take a fish off the hook, Mom," Dylan said.

"No, but I think Zach can." I nodded toward him.

Both Dylan and Noah looked over at him and slowly nodded their heads. "Can you take sunfish off? My Dad used to say they were hell," Dylan said.

"Dylan, watch your..."

Zach chuckled and held up his hand, stopping me. "I sure can. And you know what, your dad was right, they are hell. They have those spikes they love to throw just as you grab them. Hurts like hell." Zach winked.

"Can you put a worm on the hook? I can't do it because they squiggle all over," Noah said, moving some-what like I imagined a worm might.

Once again, Zach chuckled. "Yep, doesn't bother me in the slightest, and you know, maybe I can even give you some pointers and you can try putting one on with me. What do you say?"

Both boys looked over at me and with excitement shouted that they couldn't wait to go.

"Mom, can we go look for our fishing boxes?" Dylan asked.

I nodded. "Sure. I'll be up in a few minutes."

They both took off upstairs in search of the small fishing boxes I'd bought them right after their father had passed. That was the fishing trip when I learned there was no way I could put a worm on the hook or take a fish off one.

I turned to Zach and smiled. "Thank you for being so understanding and so good with the boys," I said, meeting his soft blue eyes.

"Of course. I'll be nothing but," he said, standing up, coming over to where I stood, and taking a step toward me, wrapping his arms around me, pulling me in for a hug.

The feelings that flooded my body as his arms went around me filled me with the same heat, I'd felt earlier this morning. I placed my hands against his chest and met his eyes.

"Perhaps I can teach you how to put a worm on a hook and take a fish off," he whispered.

"We will see." I smiled. "I fear I'm not very good at either of those things."

He leaned down and met my lips with the softest kiss I'd ever felt, then he pulled away and muttered something about seeing us on Sunday. When he went to reach for the door handle, I stopped him. I grabbed his hand and wrapped it back around me, and then stood up on my toes and pressed my lips to his.

Zach

I'd just finished folding a load of laundry and went to carry the basket upstairs when I heard a knock on the door. Dropping the basket, I headed toward the door. I had a lot to do if we were going with Iris and the boys tomorrow down to the lake. Sundays were normally house cleaning days, and I needed to switch them around. I pulled the door open without checking to see who was there first and came face-to-face with Valerie.

I glanced at my watch and then pulled my phone from my pocket.

"Zach, what are you doing?" she questioned, watching as I ignored her.

"Oh, I am just checking to see why I never saw the email where you gave me notice that you'd be stopping by. Remember, like you were supposed to. Yet again, I find nothing here," I said, holding up my phone. "In fact, you haven't messaged me for a long while, and you certainly didn't call and leave a message, because I just checked the machine."

I shoved my phone back in my pocket when Valerie began sobbing. She covered her face with her hands and cried. I rolled my eyes at her outburst. I really didn't have the patience for her today. It had been one thing after another with Grace, and things had gone sideways with one contractor.

"Zach, I need to talk to you," she cried.

I looked over my shoulder and up the stairs to see if Grace had heard anything. When she didn't come out of her room, I stepped out the front door and led her over to my truck, where I opened the passenger door for her. She climbed in without complaint, so I shut the door, made my way around the vehicle, climbed into the driver's seat and shut the door. I didn't need Gracie or LuAnn to hear anything.

"What is it?" I questioned with a huff as Valerie sat there crying into her hands.

"Zach, my life is falling apart. Ever since we divorced. I don't know how to fix this between us."

I gripped the wheel with my hand, my knuckles going white. I'd heard this sob story a million times before and I wasn't interested in hearing it anymore.

"Valerie, you are going to have to live with the consequences of your actions. I'm sorry, but I am not interested in hearing how tough life has become for you. I'm also not interested in hearing the things that have changed for you since Grace and I left."

"Come on, Zach, don't you have any feelings left for me at all? The mother of your child? Your wife?"

I shook my head. This was just like her. No doubt she'd had a falling out with whomever it was she was seeing now. Perhaps he too had denied her the funds she wanted to spend on something silly, just like I had.

"No, to be honest, Valerie, I don't."

"Zach, surely you don't mean that?" she said, placing her hand on my arm.

"I do," I replied.

The car grew quiet, and Valerie went back to her sobbing, while I sat there listening to her. She continued, while I only grew more and more irritated. "Valerie, what exactly does this all have to do with?" I questioned.

She sniffled and continued to cry.

"This certainly has nothing to do with me, let me tell you. It has to do with the money I won't hand over, doesn't it?"

The crying stopped, and she shook her head but said nothing, which meant I'd hit the jackpot with my question. She answered me without answering me, just like she had the night I'd finally confronted her about her affair.

"Alright, I'm going to say this one more time, so make

sure you hear me. I am not, and will not, give you money. I do not want to get back together with you, and please, for the love of everything, just call me next time."

I turned my head to meet her eyes to make sure she understood me, but she surprised me instead. In the blink of an eye, her hand was on the back of my head and her lips firmly planted on mine.

I shoved her away. "Stop it. That is enough!" Instead of listening, she grabbed me again and placed her lips on mine. "I said, stop!" I shouted, pushing her back away from me.

I climbed out of the truck, slammed the door, and made my way up toward the house.

"Zach, wait," I heard her call behind me and shut the car door.

As I continued walking away, she started sobbing again, loud enough to turn the heads of the people walking by.

"It's serious. I really need to talk to you!" she yelled.

I waved at my neighbors, but none of them waved back. Instead, they stopped walking and began looking in our direction.

"Why don't you want me anymore?" Valerie cried, putting on a full display of theatrics for everyone to see.

"Valerie, go home," I gritted between clenched teeth, doing everything I could to avoid any more of a scene being created.

"This is just like you, Zach. Ignore the needs of me, just like you do our child."

The woman was crazy. The child lived with me, and the last thing I needed was someone thinking I wasn't looking after Gracie the way I should be. I walked back to the truck, gripped her arm, and pulled her in close.

"Knock this shit off. Don't you dare claim I don't look after Grace. As for us, I've met someone else."

The look on her face was one of shock when she realized what I said. I wasn't sure if she was going to be angry or break down and cry. She stood there looking at me, and then she screamed.

"OOOOWWWWWW. You hurt me, you bastard." She pulled out of my grasp and held onto her arm.

I wanted to curl up and die as people watched. She always was good at these outbursts, at making people believe she was a victim here when, in fact, it was the other way around.

As I glanced around, taking notice of exactly who was watching, I caught LuAnn Billings on her porch looking at me. She just shook her head as she watched, likely taking in everything.

"Listen to me and listen well, Valerie. I'm going inside and I'm calling the police. Then I'm calling my lawyer. You can stay out here and throw your fit or you can get in your car and head back to wherever you are living and wait for the restraining order to be delivered, or I can have them come here and give it to you. Either way, it is up to you."

I turned around, waved over to LuAnn, and then climbed the steps of the front porch and headed to the phone.

It was a beautiful Sunday, not too hot, but nice and sunny. I was busy getting things ready for lunch while the boys and Grace were down at the water's edge digging in a small sand pit, playing games.

"I've got the food, blanket, and the pop-up shelter," Zach said, coming toward me while I watched the three kids.

"Wonderful."

I got up from my seat and helped him lay out the checkered blanket, and then we quickly assembled two of the portable pop-up shelters. Once they were set up, I began pulling things out of the picnic basket, while Zach made his way back to the truck to grab the cooler with drinks inside.

"Come on, kids, it's lunchtime," I called.

The three of them all ran over toward us, taking a seat and reaching for a sandwich each, while Zach handed out sodas to everyone before sitting down. We all took our time eating, and once the kids were done, they all took off back to the sandpit and began playing again, leaving Zach and me alone.

"You doing okay after Friday night?"

Zach had given me some space yesterday, which I'd been thankful for.

I nodded. "I am, thank you." I smiled as he slid his hand into mine.

"I have something I want to ask you."

"Okay."

"After I left the other night, I began worrying that maybe you were having regrets about things that have transpired between us since that weekend away. Especially with all the talk about how you were forgetting Lucas."

I felt my cheeks heat at his question. "I'm embarrassed to say this, but I'm not. Are you?"

He didn't answer me. Instead, he leaned over and brought his lips to mine. Instantly, I felt my body heat, and my mind wandered to each time we'd slept together. As his lips moved over mine, I wished we weren't sitting in a field with the kids only a few feet away.

"Zach..."

I pulled away almost instantly at the sound of Noah's

voice. I looked over to where they all were. Then Noah let out another yell.

Zach chuckled. "Saved by the child." He winked and got up, adjusting himself quickly. "What is it?" he yelled across the field.

"Can you help me put a worm on the hook?" Noah yelled over, now looking in our direction.

"Worms call."

I smiled as I watched Zach head on over to where all the kids were. He took hold of Noah's fishing rod and sat down on a rock and began helping him. Dylan joined them, leaving Gracie alone in the sand.

I began picking up the garbage from lunch and was just about finished when I heard a faint voice behind me ask for a drink. I smiled up at Grace. "Sure thing, sweetie. What would you like? Water or juice?"

She came over and poked her head into the cooler, then reached in and grabbed another can of pop.

"Oh, Gracie, I don't know. Your dad said earlier you could only have one."

"No, I asked him before I came over. He said it was fine. So, can you open this for me?"

I was hesitant and thought about checking with Zach first but didn't want Grace to think I didn't trust her. I was sure she wouldn't lie to me, or at least I hoped she wouldn't, so I took the can from her. "Sure."

She had just sat down and wrapped both hands

around it to take a drink when Zach barked at her, and I jumped. "Gracie, you are only to have one pop. How many more times do I have to tell you that?" he said, taking the can from her hands.

"Hey!!! Iris said I could have it," she said, frowning.

Immediately, I stopped what I was doing and glanced at Zach. I didn't want her to get into trouble, but I also didn't want there to be any issues between Zach and me. It was a tough balance because I also didn't want to accuse Gracie of lying to me.

"Oh, uhhh..." Zach looked down at the can of pop in his hand and said, "Fine, half. I'll drink the rest."

I watched as Gracie rolled her eyes, and when Zach turned his back to her to help pick up some stuff, she looked at me and stuck her tongue out at me.

I did not know how to deal with this behaviour, and I would be upset if I knew my boys behaved that way with Zach. I said nothing. I just continued packing things up.

Soon, the boys were calling for Zach again. Each one of them had a fish on their hooks. I took in their smiles as I sat with Grace while she finished her pop.

Once Zach was out of earshot, I turned and looked at Grace. "Why did you do that?"

"What did I do?"

"You lied to your father. You said I told you that you could have another pop. If he doesn't allow you to have more than one, which I heard him say earlier, why would you lie to me about it?"

"Because I can." She shrugged.

I frowned. "Grace, lying isn't a good trait to have."

She shrugged her shoulders, not caring what it was I was saying. She took another drink of her pop.

"Aren't you going to apologize?"

She shook her head. "Nope."

"Grace, I don't understand why you are being this way."

She turned her eyes on me and stared. "I don't like you, that is why."

I could feel the sting of tears behind my eyes. She may have been young, but damn, her words stung.

"My mom and dad are going to get back together. She was over at our house last night. I saw them kissing in the truck. Didn't Dad tell you?"

A wave of shock ran over me. I wasn't sure how to respond as I looked across the field at Zach, who now held onto Noah's fish in one hand, encouraging him to help hold it with one of his as Dylan watched on, rooting for his brother. I frowned. Zach had mentioned nothing to me about Valerie coming to the house. He'd simply said he thought he'd give me space. In fact, he hadn't mentioned Valerie at all.

I shook my head as I continued to watch on.

"Yep, she came by. They sat out in the car for a while,

talking, then they kissed. He was happy when he came inside the house, too. Like I said, they are getting back together."

She handed me her soda, clapped her hands together, and then got up and made her way over to the sandpit. I sat there for a few moments, watching Zach with my boys, not sure what to do with the information she had given me.

When Noah yelled over for me to look, I slowly got up off the blanket. I smiled, then bent down and picked up the blanket, folding it. Then I shoved it into the picnic basket. Then I made my way over toward the water.

Instantly, I began picking up all the boys' toys from the sand, packing them into the mesh bag I'd brought. I was just about finished when I heard the boys yelling at me to look. I glanced over at where they all stood. Noah and Dylan both held a fish in their hands, smiles on their faces.

"Look, Mom, we can do it!" Dylan yelled.

"Yeah, they are all slimy," Noah added, scrunching up his nose.

"I took mine off all by myself, didn't I, Zach?" Dylan said, looking up at him.

"Sure did, and Noah almost did. I'm sure the next one he'll have it off, no problem."

"Sure will."

I smiled but said nothing. This wasn't good. I'd introduced my boys to this man, let him in, and now, because of the information his daughter gave me, I was sure I was going to have to end things. I knew immediately that it would break their hearts if I told them we wouldn't be seeing him again.

When I met Zach's eyes, he immediately noticed the lack of happiness on my face and frowned.

"Boys, get those fish back in the water and cast out again. See what else you can catch, okay?"

They did as they were told, and Zach left them, making his way over to me. He guided me over to the closest picnic table and we both sat down away from the kids.

"Iris, what is it?" he questioned. "You don't look very good. Are you feeling okay?"

I shook my head. There was no way I could explain right now. I was too upset, and as I glanced over at where Grace was playing, I noticed she was watching us with a slight frown on her face, trying to hang on to every word we shared.

"Nothing. I think I'm just tired. It was an early morning, and all this fresh air has done me in," I lied.

"Are you sure? You look a little pale. You sure you are feeling alright?" he questioned, worry lining his face.

I nodded. "Yes. Like I said, just tired."

Grace smiled and looked down at what she was working on. No doubt she was happy that she had made me feel this way, but I still wasn't about to say anything to Zach.

"I think I am just going to get the boys and head on home."

Zach looked over at where they were fishing and then at Grace. When I glanced in her direction, she smirked, and when I met his eyes, I knew he knew something had happened. I was sure of it, but instead of making a scene, he just asked if he could help me take things to the car.

I nodded, and together we grabbed the picnic basket, blanket, and bag of toys and headed toward my car. He didn't ask me anything while we were by the car. Instead, he took my hand in his and walked me back over to the boys.

"Guys, I think it's time we head home," I called.

"Awww, Mom!" Noah cried. "I just felt a nibble."

"Yeah, Mom, we were just getting the hang of this fishing thing. Can't we stay longer and hang out with Zach?" Dylan asked, watching his bobber float on the water.

"No, I'm afraid not. Come on, bring your lines in."

Reluctantly and with sad faces, they reeled their lines in and hooked their hooks the way Zach had shown them earlier in the day. I'd turned around in time to see Zach grab Gracie and pick her up, and the five of us walked toward the car. The boys were talking Zach's ear off, which at one point would have made me so happy, but now all I could do was worry about their reaction when I told them we wouldn't be seeing him anymore.

Once we got all the kids into our vehicles, Zach stood and met me at the back of my car. "You're sure you're okay? I can bring over some dinner later if you'd like."

I nodded, averting my eyes from his. "I'm fine. I think I'll just heat up some soup and try to get to bed early."

I knew Zach was trying to read me, but I just looked away from him. I wanted to tell him what had happened, because if it were reversed, I'd want to know. Yet as I stood there, all I could think about was what if he didn't believe me? What if he took his daughter's side over mine? I really wouldn't expect anything less, and when I glanced up and saw the boys watching us out the back window, I was angry at myself for allowing today to happen.

"Is it okay if I message you later?"

"I have things to do tonight. Get lunches ready and, of course, dinner. So, if I don't respond right away, don't worry. I'll message you once I sit down for the night," I said, pressing my lips to his cheek.

Gracie and I waited until Iris and the boys had pulled out of the parking lot and were out of sight before we left. I couldn't figure out what had caused such a shift in Iris's attitude. Whatever it was, I hoped it wasn't anything I'd done.

I pulled the truck out of the parking lot and started making my way through Willow Valley. We were halfway home when I looked over at Grace, who had been oddly quiet since I'd caught her with the second can of pop.

"You have fun today?" I questioned, my eyes on the road.

Grace nodded. "It was nice."

"What did you think of the boys? They are nice, aren't they?"

"Hmm, they are okay."

"Did you notice anything about Iris?" I watched as she looked out the window and immediately shook her head.

"You sure?" I asked again. "Seems like she got a little weird after I caught you with that second can of pop she said you could have."

"Maybe she felt bad," Gracie said.

"For?"

"Saying I could have something she knew I wasn't supposed to have. You got pretty mad, Dad."

I hadn't gotten angry, not at Iris anyway. "Are you sure she said you could have the soda?"

When Grace didn't immediately answer, I pulled my truck over to the side of the road and put it into park, then turned to her and watched her.

She looked up at me and frowned. "What are you doing?"

"I'm pulling over until you answer me."

When she looked up at me, a smile formed on her lips. I knew instantly she had lied to me. Iris hadn't given her permission to have the soda. She'd lied, and whatever happened that made Iris want to leave, I had a feeling Grace had caused it.

"Grace, don't lie to me," I said, raising my voice so she knew I wasn't playing around.

"Oh, fine...I told her I could have the soda, that you said it was okay."

"You did what? You lied to me?"

Then I frowned, knowing that something as small as a can of soda wouldn't have affected Iris that way. I wondered what else had happened. I knew for a fact she would have talked to Grace the same way she would have talked to both her boys. She was a levelheaded woman. "What else did you do?"

"Nothing," she answered.

"Don't lie to me or you are going to find yourself in your room when we get home, without dinner."

Grace sat there for a minute and then crossed her arms over her chest. "I don't like her. I told her she isn't Mom."

I ran my hand over my face. "You did what? Why would you say you don't like her?"

"Because I don't. I also told her the truth."

"What truth would that be?" I questioned, fearing what I was going to hear.

"I told her that Mom was over last night and that you guys are getting back together."

I swore I saw every shade of red there was in that moment. No wonder Iris seemed so upset. I didn't have words at that moment. I just sat there, all these thoughts running through my mind.

"Where would you get an idea like that from, Grace?" I said, clenching my jaw. It was not a wonder Iris was upset.

"Because it's true. I don't like her, and I know you are

going to get back together with Mom," Grace said. "I saw you kissing in the truck last night."

I gripped the steering wheel, my knuckles going white. "You are going straight to your room when we get home, you understand? No TV, no video games, and absolutely no cell phone," I said, ripping it from her hands.

"WHAAAAAATTTTTTT?" Grace screeched at the top of her lungs. "Give it back!" she screamed.

"You heard me," I said with a raised voice as I shoved her phone in my door and pulled the truck away from the curb.

"Mom, no ifs, ands, or buts about it, she is to stay in her room the entire night. No TV, no video games, no phone —home or this one. That child needs to learn her lesson. I'm done with this behaviour. This is Valerie coming out in her, and I'll be damned if my daughter is going to act that way."

I shoved her cell phone into the cupboard above the fridge and made my way toward the door.

"She is out of control, and it's going to stop now."

"Zach, you need to calm down and take a step back for a moment. You can't go marching over to Iris's this late at night. You'll scare the poor woman. As for Grace, you can't go stomping around that way either. I agree, she was out of line and can't act like that, but—"

"Mom, please don't tell me how to raise my child. She has stepped out of line far too many times. Now, please just watch her."

"I'm not trying to tell you how to raise your daughter. However, I also don't want my son racing off like a madman and getting himself hurt in an accident or arrested. What if Iris calls the police?"

"She won't call the police, Mom," I said, grabbing my jacket and keys from the door. "New relationships are hard enough, and I'll be damned if I am going to let my eleven-year-old daughter dictate who I will and won't see."

"You know, Zach, I once recall someone else who was a problem child. Someone who once gave his stepfather grief. Her actions don't make her a bad person. This acting out means she is seeking the attention of someone."

Yes, my sister and I had been a child of divorce, and yes, we had both acted out when Mom started dating again, but we'd done nothing like this. Hell, if we had, neither of us would have sat down for a week.

"Well, seeking attention can be done multiple ways. This is not one of them. This just crossed the line. I will not stand for this behaviour, that much I can assure you. Now please, just watch her.

I headed out the door, slamming it shut behind me

and making my way to my truck. I glanced up at the upstairs window to see Grace's light on. I'd never been so angry with her as I was right now, and since I was sure it probably wouldn't be the last time, I backed out of the driveway and headed to Iris's place.

Iris sat on the front porch in a rocking chair. She held a book in her lap, her attention on the page as opposed to my truck that had just pulled up. I was glad about that, as I was sure she would have headed into the house the second she'd seen me. I climbed out of the driver's seat and shut the door, then made my way up her walkway. I was just about to put my foot on the step when she raised her eyes and met mine.

"What are you doing here?"

"I'd like to have a minute if I could."

Iris closed her book and set it off to the side and then leaned forward, her hands gripping the edge of her rocking chair. "I don't think that right now is a good idea."

Her voice was sad, and it broke me inside to know that my daughter had caused that.

"How are the boys?"

"They are finally in bed," she muttered. "It took me a while to get them settled. They were so happy about today."

I nodded. "I'm glad," I said, hoping that this might just blow over. But when I looked at Iris, her eyes fell, and she just shook her head.

"I just don't know how to break the news to them. Don't worry, I will figure it out with time. So, really, feel free to go home. No explanation needed."

She really didn't want to talk, but there was no way I could let this go on. No way could I leave her to think about all the things Grace had said to her were true. I was about to say something when she stood up and made her way to the far end of the porch and looked over the railing at the gardens below.

I followed her to where she stood and was just about beside her when she brushed past me and headed to the opposite side, doing the same thing there.

I frowned and made my way over to the other side of the porch. When she went to move, I put my arm out, blocking her.

"I just want to talk."

She lifted her eyes to mine, the hurt in them clear as she stared up at me.

"About?"

"Today. What happened?"

"There isn't anything to talk about."

I cleared my throat. "Grace told me what happened, and I'd like to start off by saying she is at home in her room with no TV, no phone, no video games."

Iris nodded. "If you think that is best, then I won't disagree, but I don't really see a reason for punishing her for telling the truth."

"Well, that is because she didn't tell the truth. She told you that her mother and I are getting back together. I don't understand where she comes up with it, but Valerie and I are over—as over as we were the day of our divorce. There never will be a us again."

Iris said nothing. She just stood there. I wasn't sure if I liked the look in her eyes. It was as if she didn't believe me.

"Grace said that she saw you two kissing yesterday."

I nodded. "She saw what she thought was kissing. Instead, what she saw was her mother trying her fucking hardest to get me to buckle in to giving her that money. What she didn't see or hear was me telling her I'd met someone."

"Why didn't you mention Valerie had come to the house?"

"I just didn't. I wanted us to have a stress-free day. I wanted things to go perfectly for you and the boys. I had no idea what went on with you and Grace, but I know her attitude toward you was not called for. She doesn't like you. She can damn well learn to like you. Also, the lying thing, playing you against me with the soda, she does this with her mother and I all the time. There will be an end to it. If you ever question anything she ever asks you or tells you, ask me. That will stop it really fast."

When she said nothing and pushed past me once again, this time sitting down on her rocking chair, I frowned. I was going to have to work to fix this, that I was sure of. Iris hadn't deserved this treatment from Grace, and I certainly didn't deserve the silent treatment from her.

"Please talk to me."

"I understand. She is probably struggling with everything. Maybe she isn't ready to share you with someone just yet."

"That isn't on her to decide. There is enough of me to go around."

Iris shook her head. "I know you think that, and before you say anything, this isn't something you did, and this isn't Gracie's fault either. I just feel that perhaps the universe is telling us something. This really shouldn't be this hard. Perhaps we are better off just staying friends."

I stood there, waiting for her to continue. I knew what she was going to tell me. That we should cut ties, so as not to complicate their lives any further and to let things run their course. If we were meant to be then we would be. She'd been pushing for that all along, and perhaps I'd been too stubborn to listen.

Was it so bad that all I wanted to do was pull her into

my arms and promise to take care of her and her boys and Gracie for the rest of my life?

The silence grew between us. Then she surprised me by walking over to me and wrapping her arms around my neck.

"Zach, I'm not your ex-wife. And you don't owe me any type of explanation. I understand Gracie is going through whatever it is she is going through. This is how she expresses herself. Our lives are messy, and just like I must protect my boys, you also need to protect Grace. That is sometimes a hard pill to swallow, believe me. I understand she needs you, and for whatever reason she is lashing out. This is when you need to be there for her. Sometimes, the hardest part of being a parent is realizing they have to come first and the things or people you really want, you can't have."

I nodded and slowly wrapped my arms around her waist. "Is that what you are telling yourself?"

She nodded. "It is. That is why I'm suggesting that we bow out of this. Not because I want to, because believe me, I don't, but because I feel you need to put your focus on Grace and figure out if you need to revisit your relationship with your ex-wife."

"I'd much rather you stay," I said, pressing my forehead to hers.

"I know you would, as would I, but I think for now it's better that I don't. I have two little boys in there that I can't risk letting get hurt again. I made a promise to myself that when I got involved with someone, they had to be happy. When I tell them we won't be seeing you again, I fear they are going to be hurt, and I need to be prepared to accept that I am the one responsible for that hurt. I am the one who hurt them. So, I'm going to say good night, Zach."

She pressed her lips to mine one last time and then without another word, she grabbed her book and her blanket and made her way inside the house, shutting and locking the door. A while after she'd gone in, I still sat on the porch, gutted that she said those words. I wished things had been different and that this wasn't the end of something that had only just begun.

Coffee and keys in hand, I was just about to leave the house when my phone rang. Irritated because I was already running late, I took a moment and looked down at my phone and saw my sister's name. She'd been calling for days, and I'd yet to answer, but since the boys were at school, I figured it may be a better time to talk.

"Hey, Beth. How's things?" I said, doing my best to sound upbeat and cheerful when I'd felt nothing but the opposite for weeks.

"Good, what about you? Have you heard anything from Zach?"

I'd told Beth everything that had happened the day of the picnic. She disagreed with me on many things, but the main one for allowing an eleven-year-old to dictate the fate of our relationship. I tried to explain it wasn't just that information I was basing it on, but when she asked me to explain myself to her, I couldn't. She told me then to put on my big girl pants, message him, and work things out or she was going to come down to Willow Valley and do it for me.

I chewed my lip. I'd messaged him like she'd asked. It wasn't my fault he hadn't responded. I cleared my throat, getting ready for her to bombard me with questions.

"No, nothing. It's been radio silence on his end."

"So you reached out?"

"I did. Twice."

"Last I checked, twice wasn't in our game plan. It's been six weeks."

Did we even have a game plan? When did we form this game plan?

"I just figured after two messages with no response to either, that the answer was clear."

"Um, the answer isn't clear until you hear a firm yes or no answer."

I shifted from one leg to the other, debating on telling her if she was right or not. At this moment, it felt like she might be. Give it another five seconds and I'd be able to tell her just how wrong she was.

"How did the boys take the news?"

I'd said nothing to them immediately after that Sunday. Instead, when they'd ask what the next adventure was, I'd told them we hadn't planned anything yet. It was easier that way until I heard from him. I was able to use the excuse that he was busy with renovations, that was until they'd come home and said that Grace wasn't at school anymore. They wondered what had happened to her, so I'd had no choice.

I thought back to night I'd sat them down and told them. I thought back to all the tears both boys had shed after I told them we wouldn't be seeing Zach anymore. In that one day, they had bonded with him so much, and I couldn't help but tear up at the thought of their faces.

"Not well. They were both looking forward to doing more fishing trips. It was my fault, honestly. I never should have taken them on that day trip."

"Why not?"

"I just should have been more careful."

The phone went quiet. "Iris, you were careful. The man was good for you, which is why I can't believe you wouldn't have let him explain."

"He did."

"I don't know about you sometimes. If he explained, then why did you walk away?"

I walked to the car and climbed into the driver's seat, doing up my belt. I had to be down at the bookstore in a few moments and really didn't want to get into this with her again.

"He may have been good for me, but the timing was off."

"Timing? Really, Iris? You told me yourself the man rocked your world. So, tell me, when is the time ever right?"

I let out a sigh. "Where did you hear that crap? When is the time ever right?" I mocked.

"Um, those were the words you said to me when I met my husband."

I laughed, remembering what I'd told her when she met him. She'd only been broken up with her boyfriend of two years for two days, and he'd come floating on in and swept her right off her feet. She'd called him a rebound, but I knew he was more than that, so I'd thrown the same words at her as she was throwing at me.

"Fine, it's my fault. He was perfect in every damn way, and it scared the hell out of me." I sniffled.

"Iris."

"What?" I said, wiping at the tears that ran down my cheeks.

I was petrified. Petrified to get involved with someone again. I'd built up so many walls after Lucas had died, and Zach had been able to break so many of them down in such a short time, it scared the hell out of me.

"Don't let a good thing go. Text him, call him, talk to him. You owe yourself that much, to at least find out what is going on."

I glanced at myself in the mirror, grabbed a tissue and wiped away any smudged makeup.

"I'll think about it. I've got to get to work."

"Alright. Have a good day, and don't forget to message him."

"You are impossible," I said, hanging up.

Thomas greeted me outside the bookstore and let me in. I thanked him, turned on the lights, flipped the sign, and started getting ready for the day. The books Trinity had ordered had come in, and so I started putting them away while she took the morning off to have her usual coffee with Peggy. I'd just gone to grab another box of books from the back when I heard the bells jingle on the door.

I stepped out front to see LuAnn Billings looking at some new releases. She often came into the store in the mornings to talk with Trinity.

"Morning." I smiled. "Trinity isn't in this morning."

"Morning. Oh, I actually came in to look for a good read."

I nodded. "Okay, well, if you need anything, just let me know." I went to grab the box when I heard LuAnn clear her throat.

"Iris, is it?"

"Yes. LuAnn, you are friends with my sister Beth, right?"

"I am."

"It's nice to meet you, aside from in passing. My sister told me to say hello when I saw you next."

"I've been meaning to call her. We have many things to catch up on. I guess I better add that to my list of things to do."

"I'm always adding things to my to-do list." I smiled as I ripped open the box and went to pull out more books, but she stopped me when she came up beside me and leaned on the counter.

"Iris, it's not like me to pry, contrary to what people think around this town, but were you dating that young man over at the bed-and-breakfast?"

I felt my cheeks flush. "We were friends, yes," I said, trying to keep my composure. I'd known that rumors had flown around town about us, and I was certain it was mostly because of LuAnn, regardless of what she said.

"Did you hear he moved back to the city?"

I shook my head. "No, I didn't." I replied.

"As you know, I live next door, and I was speaking with his mother the other day while I was doing an article for the paper on the new bed-and-breakfast, and she said he'd taken off to go back to the corporate world."

I nodded. It now made sense why I hadn't heard from him. "Well, I'm glad to hear it," I said, trying not to question what it was she was telling me.

"Yep, took his little girl and moved on back home to his ex-wife."

My eyes burned, and my throat got tight at the news. It took me a minute to accept what it was she had said. It wasn't because I was angry. If that was what he wanted, then I was happy that he had found happiness again. Everyone deserved to be happy.

"I think it was wonderful that he took little Grace back to be with her mother for her last days. It was only right that the child got to spend them with her, even if she was a pill."

I stopped what I was doing and looked over at LuAnn. She wasn't even looking in my direction. Instead, she stood there holding a book in her hand, flipping through it.

"Something of a pill?" I questioned.

"Oh, yes, the last time that woman was at the house, they had a huge blowout. That poor man, every time she appeared, it was one thing or another. According to his mother, he was having a restraining order issued when he found out the news."

"What news?"

"Oh, my dear, she was terminal."

My eyes flew up from the book cover I'd been looking at when she stopped speaking.

"Terminal?"

"Yes, she was diagnosed with a rare type of cancer and apparently needed money for treatment. His mother said he'd felt so bad that he'd denied her when he found out that he stopped the restraining order. He started paying for her treatments. When he got the news that they stopped working, he packed Gracie up and they moved home."

I made sure she wasn't looking my way and wiped at the tears that had fallen down my cheeks. I had no idea. I'd expected to hear something from him and had wondered why I hadn't, but now I knew why. He'd been too busy caring for her and for Gracie.

"I think I'm going to take this one," she said, coming over and placing the book on the counter.

I nodded and rang up her order, placed it in a bag, and the instant she was out the door, I buried my face in my hands and sobbed.

"Did you hear Brooke and Tristan entered the Festive Treasures contest this year? It was quite the event last time."

"I wonder what she will make this time?"

"Something sinful, I'm sure. I heard Tristan say he was planning on helping her. They sure turned out to be an amazing couple."

I nodded, half listening as Trinity and Peggy told me the story of how the two of them had met. I grabbed a cookie from the box they brought back and took a bite while the three of us sat in the lunchroom. My mind was still on the news I'd heard this morning, and while I was grateful for the distraction, listening to the two of them, I still couldn't keep my mind from wandering.

"Yes, it was quite something. The things he did in that bakery near drove poor Melinda crazy. She was always so frazzled while Brooke was off. It was really something to see."

"Remember how we all knew they were meant to be together?"

"Kind of how we thought you and Zach were meant to be together."

When I looked up, they both sat staring at me. "Is everything alright?" Trinity asked.

I nodded. "Just got some news this morning."

"Oh, my dear, I sure hope everything is alright?" Peggy said, looking worried.

I smiled just as the bells jingled out front. I looked at both ladies. "I'll get it. You both enjoy."

I shut the door to the lunchroom and made my way out front, only to see there was no one in the store. I frowned and made my way to the front counter to make sure the register was secured and that was when I caught sight of Grace standing just below the counter holding a book.

"Grace?" I questioned, bringing my hand to my chest.

"Hi, Iris. I really want to apologize that this book is so

late. My Dad told me to tell you he'd pay the outstanding amount when he got here."

I reached over and took the book from her hands. I remembered when she'd taken this book out.

"Well, thank you for returning it."

"You are welcome. Iris, I was wondering if I can still be a part of the reading program. I'll attend more often now, and I promise you the books won't be late anymore. Dad mumbled something about me not being able to participate anymore because of the late books."

It was then the bells jingled over the door, and I looked up to see Zach. When our eyes met, I caught the sadness in his, and then I looked down at Grace. She too had a sadness in her eyes I hadn't noticed at first.

"Sure thing, sweetie. You know where to find the books. Go take your pick, and next week we are reading *Charlotte's Web*, so you might want to grab a copy of that."

"Okay, thanks, Iris."

She slowly made her way over to the spot where we kept the books for the young reader's program, and I walked around the counter and right over to Zach, instantly wrapping my arms around him. I'd like to think it was to comfort him, but it was more to comfort me. I'd missed him so much.

"I'm so sorry," I whispered as he wrapped his arms around me. "I just heard the news this morning."

"Thank you."

"How is Gracie?"

Zach slowly let me go and shrugged. "She's doing okay, better than I expected her to."

I looked over at where she sat on the floor, cross-legged, looking at some books she'd pulled out of the shelf, giggling to herself at one of them.

"I was going to message you today," we both said in unison, causing us to laugh.

"Go ahead," Zach said, placing his hand on my lower back and guiding me over toward the counter.

"You were saying," he said, his gaze falling from my eyes to my lips.

"Well, I just heard the news this morning. I was going to message you but wasn't sure if I should."

"I'd have welcomed it. It's been hell these past few weeks. A message from you at any time would have been sunshine on some hellish days."

"No doubt. When is the funeral?"

"It was two weeks ago. We just finished wrapping some things up back in the city this week. The rest I can do from here with the help of my lawyer. We just got back into Willow Valley a couple of days ago. I had to get Grace settled at school and let her teachers know. I also had to pick up some school things or else I'd have dropped by sooner. I thought about dropping by the house last night but didn't think it would be appropriate."

I frowned. "I thought you went back to your corporate job."

Zach looked at me and chuckled. "Where on earth did you hear that?"

We both looked at one another and at the same time said LuAnn's name.

"God that woman. What other things is she spreading around?"

I laughed. "Don't worry about it. Most likely, she told me a few lies just for her benefit."

Grace came over with three books in her hands and handed them to Zach. "Can I get these, please?" she asked.

Zach looked them over and nodded. "Sure."

I made a note of the books she'd taken to mark them on the computer once they left. I handed them back to her, and she smiled up at me. "Thanks, Iris."

"Welcome."

"Alright, Grace, go get in the truck. I'll be along as soon as I pay Iris for the book that was late."

Grace took off out the door, and I looked at Zach.

"You know, don't worry about the fees," I said.

"No, that isn't how the program works, remember?" he said, winking at me.

I smiled, thinking back to the first time we'd met and how I'd given him the lecture on the rules of the program.

"I know. I'll take care of it. Don't worry."

"Iris, I'm not having you pay for my child's late return."

I glanced over to make sure the door to the lunchroom was still closed, then I leaned over the counter and met Zach's eyes. "I'll take care of it, if you'll join me for dinner, say Saturday night." The words had even surprised me, but I'd missed him, and I hadn't realized just how much until he was standing in front of me.

Surprise lined Zach's face, and then a smile fell on his lips. I wasn't sure, but I thought I even saw a hint of pink in his cheeks. "Are you asking me out?"

I smiled and pulled the book they'd returned and placed it on the counter by the computer. "So, what if I am?"

"I can't very well allow a beautiful woman to take me out for dinner."

I smiled. "Why not?"

"I wasn't raised that way. Plus, if my mother found out, she'd kill me."

We both laughed. Then he grew serious. "But Saturday sounds perfect. So, I will see you then."

I walked around the counter to walk him to the door, but as I approached him, he stopped, turned around, and pressed his lips to mine. "I really missed you."

"Missed you too," I whispered. "See you Saturday."

The next couple of months Zach, and I had talked things over in detail. We'd gone on little coffee dates, out for dinner, and a weekend away together. I'd even started helping his mother and him at the inn on the days I wasn't at the bookstore and had gone with him to a furniture store in Cedar Landing to help him choose some things for the last two rooms in the inn.

We'd also spent a lot of time with the kids either at our place or at Zachs. Tonight, we decided we'd try something a little different. Zach was taking the boys to a hockey game at an arena just outside of Willow Valley to watch Willow Valley's new team play, and while they were gone, I was taking Grace on a girls' night.

I'd just come downstairs from getting ready when I heard a knock on the door, followed by Zach's voice.

"Hey, guys! You ready to watch the hockey game?"

Noah and Dylan screamed, and I couldn't help but laugh at their excitement as they jumped around the living room.

"Hey, Grace." I smiled. "Are you ready for our girls' night?"

She shrugged, and then I caught Zach looking over at her. I'd told him it was okay if she was off occasionally. After all, she'd just lost her mother, and while I'd be there for her, I wanted him to make sure she knew I wasn't trying to replace her. "What...what are we doing?" she questioned.

I glanced over at Zach. "Well, I thought we'd go have a special dinner at The Italian Affair, then we'd head on down to Raindrops Retreat and we'd both get a manicure and pedicure."

For the first time since they'd been back, I saw Gracie's eyes light up. "Really? That sounds like so much fun."

I hadn't been expecting her reaction. In fact, I'd been nervous about hiding my surprise for fear she decided at the last minute she didn't want to go. "Great! Well, I guess we should get going. I have reservations for our dinner." I winked.

"Really?"

"Yes. They are holding a special table for us, too."

Grace smiled up at me and then ran over to her dad and wrapped her arms around him.

"Don't go too crazy with the colours on your nails. Okay," he said, hugging her to him.

"Promise," she said as she ran back over to me.

I walked over and placed a kiss on both Dylan and Noah's head as they both complained I was treating them like children when they were both so grown up.

"Have fun, be good for Zach." I laughed, ignoring them both.

"We will."

I glanced over at Zach, who then walked over and pulled me in for a hug. "Have fun," he whispered into my ear and placed a kiss on my cheek.

"You too."

With our stomachs full, we both entered Raindrops Retreat and were immediately taken into a private room. I'd specifically asked for this room, knowing that Grace's favorite colour was now purple.

She looked around, a smile on her face as she climbed into the chair and sat down. She removed her shoes and socks, as did I, and we both stuck our feet into a foot bath filled with purple bubbles.

"This is so much fun," she said as she leaned back and closed her eyes.

I smiled. "I'm glad. What colour do you want to get?"

She held her finger to her lips and appeared to be thinking hard. "Do you think they have this colour?" she asked, pointing to a purple heart on her dress.

"They might have. We will ask," I said, winking at her.

When the attendant came back, I asked her for the colours of polish they had and was given a colour ring that both Grace and I looked at together. Grace and I worked to match the colour of the heart on her dress, and I settled for a nice light almond colour.

While two girls went to work on our feet, I ordered each of us a virgin Shirley Temple and a plate of snacks that the spa offered, and we sat there snacking away while Grace told me all about how when she grew up, she wanted to work in a place like this. It was weird listening to her go on and on. After all, I was used to boys.

When the girls offered her nail decals, she looked up at me, waiting to see what I'd say. I simply nodded. She looked over the choices and pointed at a butterfly.

"That's pretty," I said, looking at her choice.

"It's for my mom. Do you think she would like it?"

She looked up at me with this look that almost gutted me. The same look I'd seen on Noah and Dylan's faces so many times. I nodded. "I didn't know your mom, but I think it's perfect."

"Me too." She smiled.

We waited patiently for the girl to put two of them on her nails. Then she looked down at her hands and smiled.

"Iris, look at how pretty my fingers are."

I smiled. "Yes, they are beautiful! I love the butterflies. They really were the perfect choice."

"What ones did you get?"

I shook my head and showed her my nails. She looked up at me with confusion. "You need a decal, too."

She tapped the lady who'd been doing her nails on the shoulder and whispered for her to get the decals again. The lady did as she asked and set them in front of her. She went over the pages of them, finally clapping her hands together. "That's it!"

I looked down to see what she had pointed to and smiled.

"Do you like them?" she questioned.

"I do," I said, tapping the sheet.

The lady carefully applied the tiny book decals to my nails, and then I held them out for Grace to see.

"It's perfect!" she said. "So you."

Once I had settled the bill and got Grace settled into the car, I walked around to the driver's side and climbed in. I'd just placed my purse beneath her feet and went to put the key in the ignition when I felt her hand touch my shoulder.

"Yes." I glanced up and over at Grace to see she had tears in her eyes.

"Oh, my dear, what is it?" I questioned, stopping what I was doing and giving her my undivided attention.

"I'm sorry. I wasn't very fair to you."

"Oh, honey. It's okay."

She sniffled and shook her head. "No, I was mean for no reason. I thought you were trying to replace my mom."

I reached around and hugged her as best as I could, thinking about what to say to her.

"That was never my plan. It's not my plan now either."

"I know that now," she whispered.

"You know what?"

"What?"

"Sometimes, when we are in a place of pain, we say and do things we wouldn't normally do. I've been there. Your dad has been there. We understand. I'm sure you didn't mean the things you said. I think you were just maybe...sad. Just like you were when your mom passed away, and like Dylan and Noah were when they lost their father, but I know there is a wonderful heart inside of you just waiting to shine, and with a little time, maybe some patience, and maybe some attention, it will be shining in no time. I also know that Dylan and Noah like you very much, as do I."

"You do?"

The look on her face was one of surprise, and it scared

me to think that a child could hold on to feelings like that.

"I do. I'd like to do this with you again, just a little girl's time. I think you need that. So, if you are open to spending the time with me, I'd be open to spending some time with you again, not as your mother, but as your friend."

Grace looked at me. Those large tears that were once there were gone, and she smiled. "I'd love that."

I stepped out of the bathroom and glanced over at Zach who was leaning against the headboard, his eyes closed. Grace and I had returned to the house, where I'd tucked her into Dylan's room, and once Zach was back with the boys, he took the time to set them up in a cool fort in Noah's room, complete with sleeping bags.

"Tired?" I questioned.

He ran his hand over his face and smiled as his eyes danced down my T-shirt-clad body.

"Maybe a little."

"Did the boys wear you out?"

Zach chuckled. "Nah."

I slipped into bed. "You sure?"

He rolled onto his side and supported himself on his forearm. "I'm positive." He brought his lips to mine and kissed me. When I felt his hand on my thigh, my body heated. I slid down farther in the bed and gripped the bed sheets as his hand found its way between my legs.

I could feel his erection pressing into my leg, and when I opened my eyes, he was looking down at me.

"What?" I quietly asked, my voice already beginning to shake as he rubbed me slowly.

"Nothing." His eyes washed over my face, then back up to my eyes. "It's just you're so beautiful when you are lost in the moment." He whispered before pressing his lips to mine.

I bit my bottom lip and closed my eyes as he continued. He pulled his hand from the space between my legs, gripped my ass, and pulled my leg over his hip as he kissed me harder. I could already feel him pressing against my entrance, and with one tilt of my hips, he slid into me.

"You feel so amazing, so tight, so wet," Zach whispered in between kissing me. "I never thought I'd feel you again."

He gripped my hair in his hands and gently pulled as he kissed my neck, while pulling me closer to him, pumping into me. I buried my face against his chest as I felt my orgasm starting to build while he held onto me, pumping hard.

"Zach, I'm sooo..."

"Go, baby, slide over that edge," he whispered, his voice raspy and rough.

He pressed his lips against mine, muting our moans as we both came.

We lay in bed, wrapped in one another's arms. I rested against his chest, my eyes closed, relishing the feeling of being held by him. He was running his finger up and down my arm like he normally did after we had sex, and I closed my eyes, enjoying the feeling of his rough fingers against my skin.

"Iris?"

"Hmmm." I opened my eyes when he didn't say anything. "What is it?" I asked, wondering if something may be wrong.

"I...I'm...I'm falling in love with you," he whispered, pressing a kiss to my neck. "Don't say anything...just let me..."

I rolled over and placed my hand against his cheek. I could see the worry in his eyes, that his affection wouldn't be returned. I placed a kiss on his lips.

"I love you too," I whispered. "I love you too."

A Year Later

"Alright, boys, you need to be on your best behaviour," I said, helping both Dylan and Noah out of back of Zach's truck.

"Awww, Mom, but tonight is going to be fun," Noah said, letting go of my hand.

"Yeah, loosen up," Dylan said, stepping up beside his brother.

I shook my head at the two of them then turned to help Grace down, while Zach went to pay for parking.

I looked up at the restaurant, The Cellar, and took it in for a moment. It was the newest place in Cedar Landing, and Zach had made us reservations after me obsessively talking about the place for months.

"I still say you are crazy booking this place. It is apparently super expensive. Tristan and Brooke ate here not too long ago. He said it almost broke the bank," I said as Zach shoved the parking slip in the windshield and locked up his truck.

"Is that why I had to wear these dress pants?" Dylan questioned, looking at Zach. "Because it's expensive?"

Zach chuckled. "Yes, that is why you look just like I do. It's a fancy restaurant, and fancy restaurants like you to dress nice."

When he'd told us he'd made reservations for us, he surprised both boys with a dress shirt, dress pants, and a little tie, Grace with a new dress, and a new dress for me as well.

"They are comfortable. Wonder if I could play baseball in them," Noah questioned, jumping around.

"Noah, enough. Now straighten up." I bent to fix his tie and straighten his pants and shirt while shaking my head as he giggled.

"Come on, guys, let's go. We are going to be late," Zach said, taking hold of Dylan and Grace's hand, leaving me with Noah.

I couldn't help but notice Dylan talking a mile a minute to Zach, but I couldn't make out what was being said. When I caught up, the chatter stopped. The hostess immediately seated us at a table in the corner by the window. We all took a minute to take in the view.

"I bet we can see all the way to Willow Valley," Grace said, looking out.

"Wonder if we can find our house," Dylan questioned, while Zach and I laughed.

"Don't think so. How about you both sit down and look at the menu," Zach said, holding a child's menu for them to look at.

Once we'd ordered, Zach poured us both a glass of wine, and I watched all their faces as I took a sip. Each one of them looked at me with a smirk on their face.

"What?" I questioned.

"She doesn't see it yet," Noah said, covering his mouth with his hands and laughing.

I glanced at Dylan, who was rocking back and forth in his chair.

"What is with you two tonight?" I asked. Then I looked over at Grace, who sat there, giving me a mischievous smile.

"Seriously, what has gotten into the three of you?" I questioned again, glancing over to Zach, who also wore a smile. "Okay, the four of you."

"Nothing." Grace smiled.

I shook my head and was about to grab my napkin when I saw a white velvet box partially wrapped into the napkin. I looked at the box, afraid to touch it, and then to Zach, who now wore a serious expression on his face.

"What is this?" I questioned nervously.

"Just say yes, Mom." Noah giggled.

"Whoa, hold on there a minute, champ," Zach said, taking hold of my hand. "Iris, this may not be the most romantic idea I've had, but I know how important the boys and Grace are to you and to me, so I only felt it was right to bring them tonight.

"It's been a roller coaster since we met—the trials, the uncertainty—but I'd trade none of it. I realized a few weeks ago just how lucky I am to be given a chance at loving again. I am in love with you and your boys. I've talked with them, and with Grace, and we all feel the same way. So, I want to ask you..."

I watched as Zach picked up the white velvet box and opened it, producing the most beautiful solitaire ring.

"Will you please be my wife?"

My vision became blurry, and when I blinked, tears ran down my cheeks. I quickly wiped them away and met Zach's eyes.

"Say yes, Mom," Dylan cried.

I glanced at Noah, Dylan, and Grace, who all sat there with smiles, and then I turned back to Zach.

"Yes!" I cried.

Zach and I both got up and hugged, then he placed a kiss on my lips before placing the ring on my finger.

We dropped the three kids off with Zach's mom and headed back to my place. We'd talked throughout dinner about the wedding. Noah, Dylan, and Grace all shared what they'd like to see. We both laughed when the boys suggested a fishing wedding, while Grace rolled her eyes.

We'd locked the house and made our way upstairs. I slipped my shoes off, while Zach took off his shirt and tie, coming over to where I stood, looking at the ring once again.

"You sure you like it?" Zach asked, kissing my neck.

"It's so beautiful," I said, still admiring the ring.

"I hope it wasn't too much, having the kids there," he whispered in my ear.

"No, not at all. Honestly, it was perfect."

"I'm glad. I'll admit, I was worried they wouldn't be able to keep the secret."

I laughed, thinking back to the looks on their faces before I'd noticed the box. "Yeah, they sometimes have a way of giving things away. Especially Noah with that grin of his."

I felt Zach's fingers gently tug at the zipper of my dress, dragging it down, exposing my back. Then I felt his fingers dance along my shoulders, slipping the dress off me.

I was still looking at the ring when he slipped the dress off my arms, and it hit the floor.

"Are you ever going to stop looking at it?" he questioned, placing a kiss on my shoulder, the heat from his body warming me.

I shrugged. "I enjoy looking at it. It's just so beautiful," I muttered.

"So are you," he whispered, his lips still pressed against my shoulder, now moving to my neck as he wrapped his arms around me.

The comfort of his arms provided a safe space for me and the boys, and I provided him and Grace the same. For two people who had endured such losses, we were both able to pick up the pieces and find love again. A love that differed from our firsts. We both knew it was because together we'd healed the scars on our hearts.

GET A FREE BOOK

Sign up for my newsletter and I'll send you a free book.

243

https://geni.us/NLSignupBackMatter

What is coming next from S.L. Sterling

Inside the Penalty Box (Vancouver Dominators # 1)
May 24th
Preorder Here: https://geni.us/InsidethePenaltyBox

Ten Minute Misconduct (Vancouver Dominators # 2)
July 23rd
Preorder Here: https://geni.us/TenMinuteMisconduct

Summer Nights and Fireflies
Coming Soon
Preorder Here: https://geni.us/SummerNightsFireflies

The Christmas Card (Willow Valley)
December 2024
https://geni.us/TheChristmasCardWV6

Follow S.L. Sterling

Did you know that bookbub has a feature where you can follow me and it will send you an alert when I release a book or put a title on sale? Sign up here and make sure you stay in the loop.

Bookbub:
https://geni.us/SLSterlingBookbub

Website
https://www.authorslsterling.com

Facebook
https://geni.us/SLSterlingFB

Twitter
https://geni.us/SLSterlingTwitter

Instagram
https://geni.us/SLSterlingInstagram

Tiktok
https://geni.us/slsterlingtiktok

Reader Group

https://geni.us/SapphiresReaderGroup

Goodreads
https://geni.us/SterlingGoodreads

Newsletter
https://geni.us/NLSignupBackMatter

About the Author

USA Today Bestselling Author S.L. Sterling was born and raised in southern Ontario. She now lives in Northern Ontario Canada and is married to her best friend and soul mate and their two dogs.

An avid reader all her life, S.L. Sterling dreamt of becoming an author. She decided to give writing a try after one of her favorite authors launched a course on how to write your novel. This course gave her the push she needed to put pen to paper and her debut novel "It Was Always You" was born.

When S.L. Sterling isn't writing or plotting her next novel she can be found curled up with a cup of coffee, blanket and the newest romance novel from one of her favorite authors.

In her spare time, she enjoys camping, hiking, sunny destinations, spending quality time with family and friends and of course reading.

To be notified of new releases or sales, join S.L. Sterling's private Mailing List.
https://geni.us/NLSignupBackMatter

Get even more of the inside scoop when you join S.L. Sterling's private Facebook group, Sterling's Silver Sapphires: https://geni.us/SapphiresReaderGroup

Other Books by S.L. Sterling

It Was Always You

On A Silent Night

Bad Company

Back to You this Christmas

Fireside Love

Holiday Wishes

Saviour Boy

The Boy Under the Gazebo

The Greatest Gift

Into the Sunset

Letting You Go

The Spencer Brooks Diaries

Our Little Secret

Our Little Surprise

Our Little Wedding

The Malone Brother Series

A Kiss Beneath the Stars

In Your Arms

His to Hold

Finding Forever with You

Vegas MMA

Dagger

Doctors of Eastport General

Doctor Desire

Doctor Right

All I Want for Christmas (Contemporary Romance Holiday Collection)

Willow Valley

Memories of the Past

The Holiday Dilemma

Letters from the Heart

My Darling Christmas

Scars on my Heart

The Happy Holidates Series

Pop Tarts and Mistletoe

Champagne and Fireworks

Summer Nights and Fireflies

9 781989 566787